FALSE
GODS

Also by Louis Auchincloss

FICTION

The Indifferent Children
The Injustice Collectors
Sybil
A Law for the Lion
The Romantic Egoists
The Great World and Timothy Colt
Venus in Sparta
Pursuit of the Prodigal
The House of Five Talents
Portrait in Brownstone
Powers of Attorney
The Rector of Justin
The Embezzler
Tales of Manhattan
A World of Profit
Second Chance
I Come as a Thief
The Partners
The Winthrop Covenant
The Dark Lady
The Country Cousin
The House of the Prophet
The Cat and the King
Watchfires
Narcissa and Other Fables

FALSE
GODS

Louis
Auchincloss

HOUGHTON MIFFLIN COMPANY
Boston   New York   London

1992

For information about permission to reproduce selections from this book,
write to Permissions, Houghton Mifflin Company,
215 Park Avenue South, New York, New York 10003.

Library of Congress Cataloging-in-Publication Data

Auchincloss, Louis.
False gods / Louis Auchincloss.
p.   cm.
ISBN 0-395-60475-3
I. Title.
PS3501.U25F34   1992   91-25571
813'.54 — dc20   CIP

Printed in the United States of America

BP 10 9 8 7 6 5 4 3 2 1

Book design by Ann Stewart

For James Parsons Auchincloss

my first grandson

CONTENTS

ARES

God of War

CASTLEDALE, in 1850, was at its zenith, the perfect residence of a Virginia gentleman. Quiet, dignified but at the same time discreetly charming, with none of the swollen pomposity of plantation manors in the deeper South, its comfortable size, its two-story red brick façade, its modest portico of four white columns with Doric capitals, seemed more to evidence a genteel welcome than any need to impress a caller. Indeed, the tobacco planted on its two thousand acres was more for the maintenance of an old tradition than a revenue necessity; Thomas Carstairs was a prosperous attorney in nearby Charlottesville with a practice that his father had had before him and that his son Roger fully expected to carry on. In Castledale the library, with its collection of Jacobean quartos and folios, was quite as important as the manager's office, and the odes of Horace, which Thomas translated for the edification of the students whom he volunteered to teach twice a week at the university founded by Thomas Jefferson, were as needful to his peace of mind as the briefs for which he was more famed.

The house was of two eras. The back part, of grey wood with a mansard roof and narrow gabled windows, dated from the late seventeenth century. The larger and grander frontal section, added in the early 1800s and designed by Mr. Jefferson himself for his friend Oakley Carstairs, was an octagon with six narrow walls and two wide ones, one of the former constituting the façade, which overlooked the green turnaround at the end of the driveway flanked by the towering box, planted according to family legend by a gardener who had once been in service to Queen Anne.

Within, a broad, paneled hallway ran from the front door to the old entrance of the ancient portion, hung with portraits of dead Carstairses, from the stiff primitives of early Colonial days, ladies and gentlemen with severe boardlike faces and unwrinkled raiment, one of the latter shown ensconced by a window through which could be seen the house in which he was presumably sitting, to the finer portraits of the eighteenth century, with the sitters' more splendid attire and more elaborate wigs and hairdos, and culminating with the magnificent likeness of Timothy Carstairs, minister to the court of Louis-Philippe, by Ingres. Roger's favorite room was the neat, still parlor, used only for company, decorated in the frilled and curlicued fashion of the citizen-king's era and dominated by a large conversation piece of the minister's children feeding ducks in a pond in the Jardin des Tuileries.

Roger knew every chapter of the family history and had looked forward, without due apprehension, to playing a role as civic as that of any of his ancestors. The most ingratiating aspect of the tribal tradition was that there had seemed little likelihood of failure for a Carstairs other than easily avoidable vices. If one had not succeeded in becoming governor or a judge or the minister to a European court, one had been equally acceptable to the hierarchy of the past by simply remaining the proprietor of Castledale. How could one lose so long as the world was sane?

So long as it was. Virginia was, but Virginia, alas, had not the sway she had formerly enjoyed. Roger in his last year at the university was vividly aware of the threats to the high civilization of which Mr. Jefferson's serene dome and noble lawn, his graceful pavilions and multitudinous columns, were the fitting symbols. The Greek calm and sense of proportion of the Virginia gentleman were rare qualities in a nation torn over slavery. Did either the arrogant advocates of secession in the deeper South or the hate-mongering Yankee abolitionists properly belong to the ordered and benignant society of which the Sage of Monticello had dreamed?

Roger and his father belonged to the school which regarded slavery as an evil that would in the course of time die out. That time, however, they firmly believed, should not be delayed by Southern fanatics or accelerated by Northern ones. It would be decided for Virginians in Richmond, not in Charleston or Boston. But Roger was unlike his fellows of the Old Dominion in one respect. He had the intense imagination that fitted his romantic looks, his raven hair and alabaster skin. He was able to imagine himself in the position of a slave in Castledale. How could *he* have endured a life without books, without philosophic discussions, without being able to wander as a student in the shadow of the university dome, without the prospect of one day being master of Castledale? And yet he *owned* human beings who had none of these things!

Roger had one classmate who personified everything he felt to be most dangerous to the peaceful solution of the ugly problem of the Southern states. Philip Drayton, of Charleston, the home of nullification, was a large handsome daredevil of a man, hearty and outgoing, but with a prickly sense of honor and the renown of having fought two duels at home, one with a fatal result, which had earned him the rhyming sobriquet of Satan. It was an apostrophe that he accepted with an easy grace — from his friends.

Drayton had transferred into Roger's graduating class from a college in his home state, perhaps, it was rumored, because of some unpleasantness related to his second duel, but he seemed bent on making his few months in Charlottesville as agreeable as possible. He was affable and charming, shedding the rays of his mildly impertinent wit and rosy puffed compliments on all classmates who came his way. Yet despite this apparent democracy of manners, it was evident that his social goal was to join, perhaps even to dominate, Roger's own clique of Virginia blue bloods. He singled out the heir of Castledale for his particular attention, with something in his air that seemed to imply that they were uniquely qualified, by birth and breeding, for the first position. Yet the strange thing about their relationship, from the very beginning, was that Roger was struck with a morbid little suspicion that in the eyes of the South Carolinian there might be room at the top for only one of them.

What soon enough emerged as their dangerous bone of contention was politics. As he and Satan were riding together on a fine autumnal afternoon over the red clay of the country-side towards a blue forest under a lemon sky, the latter extolled the glories of the old South.

"I am happy to concede that you Virginians got us all going in the first place. You provided the great general of the Revolution and the first president and much of the Constitution, though I'm not so sure the last was such a great boon. But has it ever struck you, my friend, that long years of political success may have infected you with a kind of creeping paralysis? Even here in the university, isn't there a tendency to emphasize words over deeds?"

"But universities have to be concerned with words."

"Only words?"

"No, no, morals too, of course. Ideals, aspirations, all that civilization is about."

"Civilization!" Drayton almost whistled the word. "Can't you imagine a race that has become too civilized? Sometimes I wonder whether we aren't becoming like the ancient Romans."

"And whom do you see as our conquering barbarians?"

"The Yankees, man, the Yankees! Who else in the name of Satan?" Drayton reined up his horse and leaned over to spit vigorously in the clay. "Not that they'd have the guts to strike now. But they're just sitting there, with their beady eyes fixed on us, waiting for the moment when we turn our backs, and then they'll have their daggers ready."

"I think you posit a good deal more unity in our Northern neighbors than I make out. We don't have riots about slavery as they do about abolition."

"Mebbe not yet." Drayton shrugged and rode on. "But we're still being infiltrated. Right here in the university there are men who don't scruple to say out loud that slavery as an institution is doomed."

"And it isn't?"

"No, goddamn it all, of course it isn't! Men have always had slaves. It's right there in the Bible. You see, Carstairs, you've become infected yourself with the disease. Let us pray it's only a mild case. My simple point is that Virginia, as a border state, is peculiarly vulnerable to the Yankee plague. The banner of Southern leadership must pass to the deeper South."

"To Charleston, I take it?"

"Well, what finer metropolis could anyone want? The martial spirit is very much alive and kicking in my home state."

"It's perhaps that which has caused some of its novel interpretations of the Constitution."

"You're thinking of nullification, no doubt? Well, let me tell you at once that the family of Philip Drayton, Esquire, stood to a man behind the immortal John C. Calhoun on that issue!"

Roger paused before asking, "Could the Union exist if federal laws could be voided by the states?"

"And is there any good reason, sir, that the Union *should* exist?"

"But that's treason, Drayton!"

The South Carolinian again reined in his horse. He faced Roger with a bland countenance and the twitch of a smile; his tone was very soft. "I didn't hear you, Carstairs. You didn't say anything, did you?"

Roger shrugged. "I guess not."

"Good."

Roger never doubted that the issue so created was a grave one. He did not try to brush it off as a simple case of tact and common sense intervening to avoid a dangerous and unnecessary quarrel. He knew that in a clash of wills Drayton had prevailed and that Drayton must have attributed his yielding more to fear than to caution. And wasn't he right? What was caution but fear? From now on he had to expect that Drayton would presume on his advantage to create situations, even in the presence of others, where the mask of caution would be stripped off the face of its counterpart. And there was a limit, of course, a very definite limit, to what a Carstairs could accept.

Was he to live then at the mercy of an ass? Here, in the

very shadow of Mr. Jefferson's dome, the symbol of high thinking and sober living, with the pavilions and white columns embracing the green Lawn in a clasp of Greek amity, was his mind condemned to exist in the tumult of the ass's braying? Roger groaned aloud at the idea that a whole wonderful life of books and laws and elevated thoughts, of managing the rolling acres of Castledale from the saddle of a noble steed, could be shot away by one bully's bullet. It was not the dread of physical death that agonized him; it was the cause and the folly of it.

Events promptly followed the course he had so grimly predicted. Drayton no longer sought his company alone but in groups of classmates. He would appeal in discussions to Roger for his opinions and advice, lacing his jovial flattery with increasing irony: "I wonder whether our friend Carstairs, whose worship of the Sage of Monticello may even have put him in touch with our founder's spirit, can shed any light on how Mr. Jefferson might have reacted to Mr. Sumner's extraordinary proposed solution to the so-called free soil issue?"

Drayton now revealed himself openly as the advocate of secession and frankly championed the idea of a Southern confederacy. Few of the Virginia students were ready to go so far, but the concept had its romantic appeal. The vision of a brilliant and chivalrous society, based on ancient codes of honor and aristocratic manners, caught many youthful imaginations. To Roger it was simply the essence of everything that was volatile, foolish and extravagantly violent in the Southern temperament, the poison in a society for which Mr. Jefferson's rationalism was the necessary anecdote. He waxed calmer now that his growing rift with Drayton was taking on some of the aspects of a national struggle. It would not be folly, after all, to perish for an ideal.

He was first propelled to an open disagreement with his adversary at a reception with dancing given by the rector of the university. Roger found himself in a group of stags at the punch bowl discussing a Boston riot over the recent attempt by the police to seize and return to his owners an escaped slave. Drayton, who had been drinking rather heavily, joined them and, after recognizing the topic, addressed a frankly hostile question to Roger.

"What do you say to all this, Carstairs? Isn't this nullification on the part of Massachusetts?"

"It would be if the state were rioting. But the state isn't rioting. It's trying to enforce the Fugitive Slave Law. In fact, it's the very opposite of nullification."

"Why do you always take the Yankee side? Aren't the rioters trying to nullify the law?"

"Certainly. But they are not officers of the state."

"But don't they represent an attitude widely held in the North?"

"Undoubtedly."

"Well, if so many folk both north and south are nullifiers, wouldn't it be best for the two sections to go their separate ways?"

Roger looked slowly from face to expectant face before enunciating his answer in precisely articulated syllables: "I can only speak for myself as a citizen of the Commonwealth of Virginia. I still owe my allegiance and my life to the Union so long as the rights of my state are not violated."

All eyes turned to Drayton. He seemed hesitant, baffled. Then he shrugged and turned to reach for the ladle of the punch bowl and refill his glass. The right moment had not come.

But now, like the fall of the sparrow, it *would* come.

At home in Castledale all one weekend Roger practiced firing at a target. He was a first-class shot — when his head was cool and his pulse steady. He had to train his mind as well as his hand and eye. He had to douse his hatred of Drayton with the waters of will and convert it to an icy remorselessness. For if he had to fight this man, he was determined to kill him. He would be ridding the South of a dangerous firebrand at the firebrand's own invitation.

Matters came to a head at a bachelors' party on the Lawn, at long trestle tables with candles. Drayton got very drunk and proposed a loud toast to John C. Calhoun, "the real hero of the South and the father of what we hope will one day be a new union." Roger, who knew, almost in relief, that he now had no further choice of action, remained seated while the others, even the dissenters, in tipsy good humor, drank to secession, and then rose to direct his cold tight tones to the surly Drayton. He offered a toast to the memory of "a *greater* hero of the South, the founder of our beloved university." Drayton stalked around the table to fling the contents of his glass in the Virginian's face.

For the rest of his life Roger was never quite sure exactly how it happened. At dawn, in a field in a forest some dozen miles from Charlottesville, he faced his opponent at fifteen paces before the seconds and a doctor. Drayton, sober now, had actually smiled at him, almost sheepishly, as he had strolled to his position.

"Gentlemen, are you ready? One, two, three . . ."

It has been said that a man's whole life can pass through his mind at the moment of drowning. Roger simply remembered that he heard Drayton's shot. What he was never clear about was whether he saw that Drayton had fired his pistol into the air. But all the witnesses agreed that Drayton had done so and that his basic decency had forbidden him to kill or even wound a man whom he had grossly insulted under the influence of liquor.

But Roger's recollection of what happened next was clear enough. In the three seconds that followed the retort of Drayton's pistol he had recognized with a sharp stab of relief that he was safe and had his opponent at his mercy. With frigid determination, without a nerve twitching, he took careful aim and placed his bullet in Drayton's head.

Death was instantaneous. Roger recalled the grim silence of his companions on the ride back to Charlottesville. No one congratulated him on his survival; he was simply advised to get out of the state until the matter could be settled with the police and the university.

When he returned to college after a brief suspension, he found that he was very differently regarded by his classmates. Whereas he had been formerly treated as a man of reserve, whose formal good manners were justified by his lineage and whose romantic concern with the history of his state tinged his sobriety with idealism, he was now seen as a faintly sinister figure, possessed of a cold will power that repelled intimacy. He was respected, however; courage was always admired in Virginia. Some of his old friends insisted that he had been motivated by a high principle, although they did not agree on what that principle was.

Roger himself felt no guilt at what he had done. Drayton had certainly assumed the risk, and the South was the better for the elimination of such a firebrand. But he had to face the fact that the episode had changed him, unless it had simply brought out something that had all along been concealed. He felt that he was now a man with a mission. The nature of the mission he did not yet see, but he was confident that time would bring it out. He did not for a minute believe that he had killed a man for nothing.

Girls were especially awed by his new reputation; his good looks were now described as Byronic. His reticence and solitary habits added to his fascination, and to Kitty Cabell, the prettiest debutante of her Richmond season, he seemed the Corsair himself. Roger had known Kitty since childhood; they were even, like so many of the first families, related, and he had long been perfectly clear that she had the characteristics, both good and bad, of the renowned Southern belle. She was superficial and affected, and she posed as being a good deal sillier and less worldly than she was, but she was also enchanting. She now turned her full lights upon him and soon aroused his lust to the point where he was reluctantly willing to pay society's price to sleep with her. They were married in 1855, shortly after his father's death from a stroke, and settled in Castledale.

Kitty proved one of those rare persons who become perfectly amiable when their ambition is satisfied. As chatelaine of Castledale and mother of a small son, she happily took the lead in the local society and got on splendidly with her docile mother-in-law, who continued to live in the house. That Roger, engaged in his law practice and the supervision of the beloved plantation, should be little concerned with her she accepted as the conventional attitude of a husband. So long as his manners were correct — and they invariably were — she was content with her bargain. But no more children came, and in time he requested his own bedroom. If he ever had an affair, she never learned of it, and that was all she cared about. As for herself, there was never any idea of a lover. She was afraid that Roger might have killed him.

Everything would have been well enough, in Kitty's opinion, had the Yankees only seen fit to leave them alone. She had spent much of her youth in Paris, where her father had represented a syndicate of tobacco planters, and she had viewed with a detachment imbued in her by her older brother Lemuel, a satirical dilettante, the semiludicrous efforts of their Francophile parents to be included in the *gratin* of the old faubourg. Lemuel had taken a perverse delight in establishing his dominance over his pretty younger sibling by exposing the silliness of a father who spent an hour every morning practicing his French *r* and of his mother, who thought she would ingratiate herself in legitimist circles by dressing as closely as she could to the Empress Eugénie. He made Kitty understand that Vielle France, however polite, however *amicale,* was never going to clasp to its bosom or allow to marry one of its sons an American girl who wasn't a Catholic and who hadn't a fortune, the plantation at home being morally entailed to the firstborn, a brother older than her and Lemuel. Kitty learned that in a foolish world one had to rely on oneself, and she didn't forget this when the family returned to Richmond. She had no greater loyalty to slave-holding Virginia than she did to the Faubourg St.-Germain. She laughed at the golden calves on both sides of the Atlantic, but she was always careful to laugh to herself.

Roger's attitude to the great issue of the day struck her as just as senseless as everyone else's. He believed that the slaves should be freed, but he was quite willing to kill anyone but himself who proposed to free them. At least that was how it looked to her. He disguised his fierce ego, as she saw it, behind the mask of a Virginia patriot. And after the abortive John Brown raid onto his sacred state's soil, he became as hot a secessionist as the fiery South Carolinian whose brains he had blown out.

In the first years of the fighting, during which she had to manage a crumbling plantation while he was off, all over the state, with Jeb Stuart's cavalry, she sometimes complained to her mother-in-law that the wives and mothers of warriors had the worst of their wars.

"Let us call it our glory," the docile widow would invariably reply.

2

Hate sustained Roger during the whole of the conflict, hate and, at least in the first two years, his hope that the Confederacy's choice of Richmond as its capital might restore Virginia to the leadership it had enjoyed in the golden days of Mr. Jefferson. No compromise, he always insisted grimly, was possible with the enemy that was ravaging his native state. Although he met some captive Union officers who he had to concede had shown at least the courage of gentlemen, he could only pity them as the tools of an unholy alliance between fanatical abolitionists and avaricious war profiteers. And when, after two years of constant campaigning, he was offered the relief of a staff job in Richmond, accompanied with a promotion, he turned both down to continue in the cavalry. Nothing else seemed to make any sense to him.

The double defeats of Vicksburg and Gettysburg destroyed his last illusion of ultimate victory for secession. No matter how many battles or skirmishes his company won on mangled Virginia soil, no matter how horribly its rich beloved red clay seemed to ooze Yankee blood, there were always new waves of the boys in blue rising out of the very foam of their collapsed predecessors.

He had no wish to survive the inevitable end. He was wounded three times but always slightly; he seemed to be proving the old adage that death avoids those who seek it in battle. The long days in the saddle riding through familiar countrysides, sinister now in their haunting beauty, the nights in the field where he would let his exhausted body drop to the earth after swinging the lead ends of his blanket around his shoulders, began to produce an odd consolation in their very monotony and dreariness. Once when he sat up till dawn couching in his lap the head of a boy whose lifeblood was slowly dripping away, he felt something like peace at his own acceptance of all that the loathed enemy had destroyed. But he could not bear the sight of Castledale; on one of his leaves he put up at a hotel in Richmond rather than go home. And when word reached him that his mother had died, he could only be thankful for what she had been spared.

After Appomattox he had the privilege of a few words with General Lee, who had stood as godfather to his son seven years before. Like all the army he worshipped Lee, but he was ready to relegate him to the past. "Go home, my friend," the general said. "Now the real task awaits us. God helping, we shall not shirk it."

Roger nodded and went home, but he stayed there only a year. He felt like an atheist who has died only to discover that there *is* an afterlife. It might not be a better one, but at least he would be free of the old.

"I'm going up to New York to see whether I can make a living there practicing law," he informed his younger brother, Ned, a mild and gentle man, a bachelor, who deemed it entirely fitting that he should fall in with all of Roger's schemes. "Look after Castledale and Kitty and the boy. If I don't starve, I'll send for them when I can provide them with a home there. Explain this to Kitty tactfully after I've gone."

A cousin of his mother's had married a well-to-do New York landlord, Basil Tremont, a generous victor, who had answered Roger's letter of inquiry with the assurance that he would help him at least to a modest start.

Roger's cousin had a small office on Canal Street, where he and one old clerk and an even older female secretary handled the Tremont family affairs, largely the collection of tenement rents, and he accorded his Southern relative a narrow cubicle, used for file storage, as his "chambers." But it was free, and although there was no question of Roger's getting his hands on the family law business, he did receive an occasional crumb from that ample table in the form of a small eviction or lease renewal. Furthermore, Basil Tremont was good enough to tout these services to the guests at the Sunday night suppers in Union Square to which Roger was occasionally invited, and he thus picked up some modest retainers, enough, anyway, to pay for his bedroom in Houston Street and his simple meals.

He used his plentiful spare time, both day and night, in studying New York cases and statutes in the library of the Manhattan Law Institute. He had no interest in the social scene or in public amusements. He heartily despised the whole dirty brown noisy city with its Yankee twangs and its Yankee familiarities. He had come north for one purpose only, the recoupment of his fortune, and his eye was rarely averted from that goal. But he perfectly realized that this could not be accomplished by law alone, and he was careful to cultivate the few important men he met at the Tremont Sunday gatherings.

The talk there, however, was dominated by the women, whose importance Roger recognized but did not exaggerate. Mrs. Tremont, a vast cheerful bundle of flesh and red velvet, could get anything she wanted from her pale bald spouse, but she wanted things only for herself and her offspring. She and her fellow matrons had not the smallest interest in business or politics; the power they sought and achieved was purely domestic. They had, of course, the power to ruin a man with their tongues, but any such danger was easily averted by a routine exhibition of Southern gallantry. They were rather titillated at meeting a handsome and impoverished rebel officer; they enjoyed the idea of exercising a beneficent open-mindedness in their affable condescension to a safely defeated enemy. If Roger had been free, he might even, with a skillful play of his few trumps, have secured the hand of one of their well-endowed daughters. As it was, he had to direct his principal attention to the men.

The City Club, a large pink-and-white building on Madison Square with a membership of lawyers, judges and politicians, was more useful to him. The ever-generous Basil had treated him to a year's guest membership, and it was an easy enough matter for a former Confederate officer, dropping into the big bar with the oak-paneled walls and potted palms, to fall into friendly converse with those members who had served in the Union Army and evoke the bond between fighting men that never quite includes even the bravest noncombatant. Roger, in postmortems of battles, was always careful to avoid any criticism of Union strategy. His cool good manners, unaffected by the few drinks he permitted himself, made him popular, and after his year's free membership was up, he found it renewed for another without dues. When he went to the treasurer's office to inquire about this, he was politely shown a minute from a meeting of the board of directors stating that Colonel Carstairs could pay dues "when his ship came in."

Roger decided to accept this. He would not have done so in Richmond, but then Richmond was reality, a quality he was not willing to accord New York.

The president of the club, Charles Van Rensselaer Pratt,

turned out to be just the man he had been looking for. He was every inch a gentleman — at least, as Northerners defined that term — tall and grave and dignified, with a short, well-cut beard and dull blue gazing eyes under bushy eyebrows which seemed to be wondering whether you were as much a gentleman as he. His Knickerbocker background would have qualified him more for the presidency of the Union than the City Club, but Roger had heard that his intense patriotism during the war, throughout the whole of which, like Roger, he had fought, had prompted him to resign from an institution some of whose most distinguished members had favored a compromise peace. Pratt at forty looked ten years older, as fitted the senior partner of the Wall Street firm that his late father had founded, and his reputation for honor and high-mindedness was unchallenged. The same, however, could not be said of some of his partners. There were even those who dared to suggest that he was a figurehead of respectability to be displayed in nobly speechifying meetings of bar associations and behind whose broad and stylishly tailored back a good deal of less edifying but profitable business was transacted.

Pratt was intrigued by what he called Roger's decision to "move his career north." He visited the club regularly on Monday nights, when his wife dined with her invalid mother, and made his two whiskies last for two hours. He soon made it a habit to invite Roger to join him at his reserved table in a corner of the barroom. They would talk of problems facing the South and what Pratt called its "future redemption and regeneration." Roger, for whom whiskey had become a controlled solace, found that it increased his tact by temporarily softening his bitterness. He was not even tempted to call the club president an ass.

"Oh, I suppose the South will come back in a way," he

conceded as he puffed his pipe, for he smoked now too. "But it will not be in any way that will interest me. I have seen the old days, and there can be no possible revival of *them*."

"But surely in time the great plantations will revive. Will it make such a difference to you that the hands will be paid instead of owned? Mightn't they even be more efficient?"

Roger smiled inwardly at this hint from the counsel to capitalists. "It's not that, sir. I belonged to the civilization that died at Appomattox. I do not care for reconstructions."

"So you will stay here?"

"If I can survive here."

"And bring your family north?"

"In time."

"How do you think they will like it here?"

Roger smiled again, this time outwardly with a touch of grimness. "Kitty will like it, if I can buy the things she wants. The boy, I suppose, will grow up a brave little Yankee."

"And what about your place? It's called Castledale?"

But Roger was not ready to discuss Castledale with even a well-meaning Yankee.

"My brother will take care of it."

"Well, I'm sure that our divisions will heal sooner with men like you in our midst. Men who have fought with courage and conviction for a cause in which they seriously believed."

Roger treated himself to a long sip of whiskey in answer to this. Nothing could be allowed to impede him from finding an opening in Pratt's firm. When he spoke, it was to give the topic a new twist. "Does it ever occur to you that the real winners of the conflict in which you and I battled so long and hard were not the soldiers at all, but the ones who had the wit to stay home?"

Pratt's blue eyes took on something like a spark. "You mean the dastardly profiteers?"

"I mean all those who put business ahead of war. How many of your veterans do you see in the entourage of the new president?"

Pratt's sigh was windy. "Very few indeed, I fear. General Grant seems to have forgotten his old comrades. I cannot see what *he* sees in market speculators of that type."

"If we fighting men would stick together, we might have a chance to run the show."

"Do you know, sir, I *like* that idea! And do you know that of the ten partners in my firm I am the *only* one to have worn the blue uniform?"

Roger raised his glass. "To the blue and the grey!" He just managed to suppress a laugh as Pratt smote the table with his fist in his enthusiasm.

Roger had a project for Pratt on their next meeting. He had been reading in the newspapers about the struggle of the New York and Albany Railway Company to corner the stock of the Ontario line, a client of Pratt's firm. He had obtained copies of all the briefs in the various lawsuits involved and studied them carefully. On a Monday night at the City Club he expounded a plan of defense to Pratt that was so simple as to have escaped the attention of the lawyers on both sides.

"I note that the Albany line has succeeded in obtaining an injunction from Judge Barnard of the Supreme Court of New York County prohibiting Ontario from issuing more stock for any reason. I fail to see the basis for so sweeping an order."

"The basis, I fear, may lie in the venality of His Honor. The Albany line is stronger with the city's judiciary than we seem to be."

"The *city's* judiciary. What about trying a judge farther north? In Sullivan County, say, or Columbia?"

"But what have they to do with us?"

"As much as any of the supreme courts in Manhattan.

Doesn't each supreme court have plenary jurisdiction throughout the state?"

"Hmm. That is so, isn't it? But why should upstate judges
interfere in matters that don't concern them?"

"You could make it their concern."

"How?"

"How did your opponents do it?"

"You don't mean we should bribe them?"

Roger laughed so that he could retreat into a joke if needed.
"Think how much cheaper an upstate country judge would be
than one of the gorged jurists of our opulent town!"

"Carstairs, what are you saying?"

"How many of these black gowns were fighting men,
Pratt?"

Pratt looked at him gravely and then chuckled. He too
would treat it in jest. "Still, the idea of petitioning an upstate
judge is interesting. I'll discuss it with my partners. After all,
we might find one who would be glad to correct an injustice.
Yes, why not? It is certainly a novel idea."

Pratt took the matter up with his firm, and the very next
day Roger was summoned to the office of the partner in charge
of litigation, Carl Gleason, a ferret-faced little man whose
nervous fingers roamed like spiders over the silver objects on
his desk while his cold eyes remained fixed on his visitor.
Having heard Roger's exposition, he wasted no time in offering him a job as a clerk in Pratt & Stirling. But he was clearly
a bit taken aback by how hard Roger bargained over salary;
obviously he was dealing more with a fighting colonel than a
starving ex-rebel attorney. When they came at last to terms,
he issued this parting warning: "I trust it is quite understood
that you are working for me and no other partner. And no
other partner includes even Mr. Pratt. I am always very particular with that in litigations."

Roger nodded. He quite understood. There were things he might have to do that the senior partner was not to know about. That the senior partner might very well not *want* to know about. And indeed his very first job was to journey north to the township of Ayer in the county of Clinton to consult one Supreme Court Justice Owen, whose initial reluctance to exercise his injunctive powers in favor of Mr. Gleason's client was overcome by an envelope passed silently across his desk.

Thereafter it was always Roger who took care of what Gleason called the "delicate side" of litigation. His salary was increased twice so that after only two years he was able to bring Kitty and young Osgood north and lodge them in a brownstone on Brooklyn Heights. And only two years after that he presented himself one morning before Gleason's desk and coolly demanded to know whether the time had not come for him to be made a junior partner in the firm.

"But you're paid as much as a junior partner now!" Gleason protested. "I thought you were too great a Virginia gentleman to care about our Yankee partnerships."

"Why I care should be obvious to a lawyer as smart as yourself, Mr. Gleason. An associate can always be dumped. I do not wish to be dumpable."

"And if I refuse?"

"And if I go to the Commodore?"

Commodore Vanderbilt was then busily engaged in trying to corner Ontario stock. A former clerk of Ontario's counsel, particularly one who had handled "delicate matters," would find rapid employment with the old pirate.

"Are you trying to blackmail me, Carstairs?"

"The definition is yours. All I ask is fair treatment. We sink or swim together."

"Jeff Davis shouldn't have wasted you in the cavalry. If he'd had you in his cabinet, treason might have prospered."

Roger stiffened. "In the old days I'd have called you out for that. But now may I simply remind you that secession was not treason until established by *force majeure*. And that President Davis, as we referred to our chief executive, would never have stooped to your ways of doing business."

"*My* ways!" Even the hardened Gleason gaped at this. "Well, of all the nerve!" But he was not a man to make an issue out of inevitable things; he even managed a grin. "You'll never believe it, Carstairs, but I was planning all along to make you a partner."

"Of course I don't believe it. But shall we agree that I'm to be a member of the firm as of the first of the month? We can discuss my percentage later."

Gleason threw up his hands. "I agree."

3

Roger not only became a partner. Ten years later, when Gleason died of a stroke, he succeeded to his position as chief of the department with a higher percentage of the firm's profits than the nominal senior partner, Charles Pratt. The older and more distinguished members of the bar may have been disturbed by rumors of his methods of convincing the judiciary, but the tolerant and cynical laymen of the day took for granted that he was probably little worse than his fellow attorneys.

Roger neither made nor sought to make friends in New York. His manners were polite but formal; he asked nothing of his partners or clients beyond completion of the particular business at hand. Kitty, on the other hand, was strikingly successful. She bloomed in Manhattan society and charmed everybody with her revived Southern belle manners. She was as open and witty as he was silent and grave; she dressed and talked well and entertained delightfully in the brownstone mansion of her dreams that Roger had built for her on Murray Hill on condition that he would not have to preside at her parties. For that he summoned north her bachelor brother Lemuel, even more of a dilettante than in his Paris days, and bought a literary gazette for him to edit when he was not escorting Kitty about the town. Society much preferred the genial Lemuel to the austere Roger, and the brother and sister were soon among the most popular couples in Gotham. Much as Roger scorned Kitty's social success, he was too just not to recognize that it ill became a husband who had brought his wife to a strange city to begrudge her her adaptability to its ways.

He gave Kitty what she wanted, but he gave even more to the re-embellishment of Castledale. His brother Ned, too self-effacing to occupy the main house and contenting himself with the old overseer's lodge, lovingly supervised the restorations ordered by his senior: the cleaning and stretching of family portraits, the affixing of new panels to interior walls and new bricks to the outer ones, the installation of plumbing and central heating, the replanting of the gardens and box, and, most important of all, the arrangement, against appropriate settings of new curtains and carpets, of the beautiful Colonial and early Federal furniture and porcelains purchased by Roger at auction sales of the grand old mansions of the South. For if he thus seemed to join the plunderers of the Confederacy, it was only to bring together the finest of its treasures in a museum to be devoted to its memory and to be paid for with Yankee dollars.

This, of course, had to be the justification of everything he had done since Appomattox. His only happy times were the occasional weekends he spent at Castledale, roaming the rooms and corridors and riding over the grounds. Kitty never accompanied him, claiming with undeniable truth that he would rather be alone with his "true love," but in the first years of the restoration he had sometimes taken Osgood. The poor boy, however, was not only plain and stout; he was hopelessly dull. He had at an early age given up trying to curry favor with the stern father of whom he stood in helpless awe; he seemed to divine that it was not within his limited range to gain paternal affection or even approval. Yet Roger sometimes reluctantly suspected that his son would have given anything to be loved a little. Kitty was a demonstrative but easily distracted mother, and the smallest amount of warmth from a taciturn and preoccupied male parent might have made all the difference to the lad. But every time Roger resolved to pay him a little more attention, the boy would irritate him with some odious Yankee expression or demonstration of his ignorance of Southern history and tradition, and at last he resolved to take him south no longer, justifying the decision with the reminder that, after all, he intended to convert Castledale to a museum and sanctuary where Osgood would never have to live.

Ned Carstairs did not approve at all of what he dared to call his brother's demeaning of his nephew, and he stepped out of his usually subservient role to argue roundly that Osgood was the rightful heir to Castledale and should be trained to be a good proprietor. But Roger was not accustomed to taking advice, and least of all from Ned, and he simply shrugged in answer. And so it was that Osgood played little part in his father's life until the night when, aged twenty-four, a bank clerk still living at home, he penetrated the usually forbidden-to-all area of the paternal study to announce that he was engaged to be married. Roger, surprised for once, looked up at the round serious eyes in the round pale face of his only child and felt a pang of remorse that he should not have the least idea of who the young lady might be. In his confusion he took refuge in sarcasm.

"I trust, anyway, not to a Miss Gould or a Miss Fisk."

"Oh, no, Father. To someone you will really approve of."

"Heavens! Do you mean a Virginia girl? I didn't know you knew any."

"Well, no, but perhaps the next best thing. She's the daughter of one of your partners."

Roger was on his feet before he was even aware he had moved. "Good God, not to one of Gleason's girls!"

Osgood looked bewildered by such violence. "Oh, no, sir, I don't even know them. It's Felicia Pratt."

Roger stared. He seemed to recollect a large placid goose of a maiden. "Charles Pratt's daughter?"

"Of course. Isn't that all right?"

"What does *he* say?"

"I don't know. I haven't spoken to him yet. I wanted to get your approval first."

Roger rubbed his brow, wondering how much more there was that he didn't know about this young man he had found so dull. He turned away now from Osgood's anxious expression. He could hardly face the idea of the vexation that a belated regret for his paternal indifference might cost him. It was simply too late, much too late, to establish any real relationship. "Well, if Charles doesn't mind, why should I? You must bring Felicia to the house so that your mother and I may meet her."

"Oh, Mummie knows her and likes her ever so much!"

"Then there you are." Roger contrived a smile. "She must be all right."

4

Kitty Carstairs on a dark snowy evening in the winter of 1882 was seated before the dressing table in her pink-and-yellow Louis XV boudoir on Murray Hill, dressed already, as she liked to put it, *en grand gala du soir* and attaching to her lobes the ruby earrings that went with her scarlet crêpe de chine. On a chaise longue by the window lounged her brother Lemuel, languid and splendid in white tie and tails, whom her maid had just summoned up from the parlor.

"Charles and Jane Pratt will be at the Mortimers' tonight. I've asked Clara Mortimer to seat you next to Jane."

Lemuel threw up his arms in disgust. "Just because I couldn't take you to the Sykeses' on Friday? Really, Kitty, how vindictive can a sister be?"

"Bore Insurance should pay you three hundred for her."

Kitty and her brother paid dues to a small private group which listed the biggest bores in Gotham and paid off at so much a head to any member who found himself stuck beside one at a dinner party.

"But it's cheating if you arrange it with the hostess! I'm surprised at you, Kitty."

"*I'll* pay you the three hundred then."

"Happily, I have no prejudice against taking money from a woman."

"It's a comfort that I can always depend on your being devoid of senseless male inhibitions."

"I'm not such an ass, anyway, as to take *that* for a compliment. But tell me what you want me to do with the sublime Jane Pratt. Not make love to her, I trust?"

"Could one? No, I simply want you to convince her that Osgood is in no way like his father. Charles Pratt is actually objecting to the match. He doesn't fancy his beloved Felicia as Roger's daughter-in-law."

Osgood sat up. "His own law partner?"

Kitty shrugged as if the vagaries of the male sex were beyond her. "It seems he objects to Roger's ethics."

"Well, I certainly can't blame him for *that*! But what about his own?"

"That's what Osgood asked. The poor boy is in a terrible state. He had no idea that Roger wasn't like any other lawyer."

"That's the trouble with New York. He is."

"Now, Lem, don't be pompous. I haven't asked you to hold forth on the evils of modern society. Pratt apparently told Osgood that he had stayed with the firm after Roger became a partner only to counteract his 'bad influence.' "

"And to make a very good living as he did so!" Lemuel clapped his hands and hooted. "I'm only sorry the great Dickens is not alive to put Pratt in a novel. He would excel Mr. Pecksniff as the archetype of hypocrisy. Has Roger heard of this yet?"

"No! And he mustn't or he'll blow us all to Kingdom Come! That's where you come in. I have almost persuaded Jane Pratt to talk her husband out of his silly attitude. I count on you to put in the finishing touches."

"Is it really worth it? I'm not at all sure that Osgood couldn't do better than the Pratts. I was hoping he might catch a real heiress from one of the families that are still climbing. A Vanderbilt, for example."

"No, no, I know where we are socially, my dear. The Pratts are just right for us. It's all very well for you, a bachelor, to talk about our doing better. It's easy enough for you to go anywhere you like. But for a woman it's different. There are plenty of dowagers in this town who are ready to do me in if given half a chance. My success has aroused envy, and don't fool yourself that that war has been forgotten yet. And even if it had been, Roger's snooty attitude about Yankees would revive it. If we had a real showdown with a couple as respected as the Pratts, it might upset my applecart!"

Lemuel appeared to be weighing this. "Well, I suppose there may be something in what you say. Jane Pratt *is* a descendant of Peter Stuyvesant, though I doubt if half the new families even know who he was. How do you want me to approach her?"

"What I really need is to get her to make Charles drop his condition."

"A condition to his consent to the wedding?"

"Yes. It's a very stiff one, I'm afraid."

"What *is* Charles's condition?" came a voice from the doorway, and they both turned to face Roger. Kitty's self-possession rarely deserted her. "Oh, a silly condition," she replied casually, as if relieved that his arrival had saved her the trouble of sending for him. "You know what a stickler Jane is in matters of etiquette. Apparently they're in mourning and don't want to have a wedding reception."

Roger's expression was dangerously impassive as he advanced into the room. "For whom are the Pratts in mourning?"

"Oh, I don't know. Some old cousin three or four times removed. I told Jane that we didn't care about a reception. That we'd give a party for the bride and groom after the honeymoon."

"Just a minute, Kitty. One doesn't forgo a wedding reception for one's only daughter because of the death of a distant cousin. Even for a close relation, one would simply postpone the wedding for a month or so."

"Oh, Roger, you know these old New Yorkers. They mourn for years for the remotest kin!"

"Do they? I saw Charles in the office this morning, and he was certainly not wearing a black tie or even a mourning band. In fact, I particularly noticed his very red cravat." And then his features suddenly hardened. "They're not in mourning at all, are they, Kitty? Not even for a cousin twice removed?"

"Well, maybe they just don't like wedding receptions!" Kitty exclaimed with finely affected exasperation. "*You* should be glad anyway. You hate the damn things and probably wouldn't even go to it. And as for me, the only thing I'd like about it is it would probably bust our Bore Insurance Society!"

But Roger was inexorable. "The reason Charles doesn't want to give a reception is that he doesn't wish to introduce his friends and relations to me. Isn't that it?"

"Oh, Roger, what if it is? What do we care? We don't have to marry *him,* do we?"

"But I care very much. And I shall look forward to having a general clarification with Charles Pratt no later than tomorrow. It will be my pleasure to inform him that if he feels ashamed of this alliance, *I* feel degraded. I shall further inform him that he has been paid by his partners through the years, not for his legal aptitude or his roster of clients, both of which are, to say the least, exiguous, but for his constituting the formal façade of piety which all good Yankee enterprises require."

"Oh, that's just fine!" Kitty rose and faced him with clenched fists. "What fun you're going to have! You'll smash poor Osgood's wedding and maybe even break up your law firm. You'll have all New York society shouting for your head. And best of all, you'll bring me down in the general wreck! That's what you've always wanted, isn't it? Well, go ahead and try! I dissociate myself from you. Osgood and I will make it alone."

"I shall always support you, Kitty."

"I don't want your Yankee money!" she almost shrieked.

But this was too much for Lemuel, who now rose and glanced at his watch. "If you don't mind my interrupting this little scene, Roger, Kitty and I must be off to the Mortimers'. I believe we shall meet the Pratts there."

"Tell Charles I shall come to his office in the morning" was all that his brother-in-law grimly replied.

5

The two years following Roger's rupture with his firm, which resulted from the irate Pratt's demand that their partners choose between the two of them, he spent alone in Castledale. Kitty remained in the New York house, which he supposed she would be able to maintain for a few years on the half of his savings that he had turned over to her. After that he had little interest in what happened. He no longer had any earned income, and the remainder of his capital was destined for the endowment of his museum. It was not a great sum, at least by the standards of the new rich, but costs in Virginia were still low, and, his foundation once legally established, he could move into the old overseer's lodge with Ned. But for the time being he was occupying the big house, a moody hermit amid the splendors of his continued restorations.

He saw almost nobody but his ever-sympathetic brother. The local gentry would have been glad enough to welcome him had he taken the trouble to ingratiate himself, but his aloofness was repelling, and in time the rumors of the bad reputation that he enjoyed even in a city as wicked as New York began to tarnish his image. When, in addition, the respectable neighbors learned that he had deserted a blameless wife and was planning to disinherit a dutiful son, they dug up the old legend of his duel with Drayton and converted it to something more like a cold-blooded murder. It was even claimed that he had known ahead of time that his victim intended to fire into the air.

Roger cared little for their prattle, some of which the more troubled Ned related to him in the vain hope that an ameliorated attitude might appease the countryside.

"But don't you see, Ned, that what they're saying about me is basically fact? Oh, they've added a lot of nasty and false details, it's true. People wouldn't be people if they didn't do that. But I can't quarrel with the main outline of their image of me. I *am* a bit of a monster, you know."

The only criticism that he did mind came from within the walls of Castledale, not from humans, for nobody lived there at night but himself and only the cook and parlor maid by day. It came from ghosts. The pale wooden faces of the Colonial Carstairses over coats and dresses as unwrinkled as planks, looked not at him but past him. The Revolutionary general, whose big nose and alarming sabre dominated the dining room, saw him but did not recognize him. And his mother, looking sad and subdued even as a debutante in the day of Andrew Jackson, seemed to be conveying the timid message that she couldn't talk to him now, before the others, but could she have a word with him later, alone? Yet the note the family appeared to be striking was not one of hostility, or even, really, of disapproval. It was more that he didn't belong there. He had called at a house where he wasn't expected. What did he hope to gain by prolonging the error?

"They want me out of Castledale," he told Ned one day at lunchtime, waving towards the portraits on the wall. "They treat me like a stranger. Even an intruder."

"How ungrateful of them! After all you've done."

"Oh, they don't care about that. They'd rather be shabby.

They feel about me the way the Stewarts down the road feel about the rich Yankee who bought High Farm."

"But Castledale is *yours,* Roger!"

"Not in their opinion. I've forfeited my rights."

Ned's finger rested on the base of his wineglass as he pondered something. "There's one way you might bring them around."

"I know. By willing the place to Osgood. You're a stuck whistle on that subject. But he couldn't keep it up, even if he wanted it."

"He could if you left him the money."

"There's not enough. He'd use it for his family, and it'll be needed to maintain the house. Osgood hasn't a penny over his wretched salary. Pratt cut off Felicia when she married without his consent."

"He'll forgive. They always do in the end."

"But he's damn near bust himself! Osgood wrote me about it. Pratt was always the world's worst investor, and he got his ears pinned back in that Montana mine fraud."

"Oh, so Osgood writes you?"

"When he's desperate. Felicia had twins, you know. Oh, I sent him a check, of course. I'm not quite the ogre people say. But the real money has to go to the museum. You know that, Ned."

"*I* don't know it. You may. I have no use for museums, at least in the country. Castledale should be owned by a Carstairs."

One night, after a solitary dinner, Roger had risen and strolled to the fireplace to take his usual leave of the portrait over it of General Carstairs. He would offer his great-grandfather a miltary salute, but he never went so far as to imagine that it would be returned. But that evening he had a curious feeling that it had been, that the hero of the Battle of Chesnut

Hill, in view of some special and perhaps ominous occasion, was offering him a recognition that might never have to be repeated.

And then the blankness returned to those authoritative features, and Roger felt, in a swirling, diving emptiness, that he himself was no longer there.

When he regained consciousness he was in his bed, and Ned, standing by it, was telling him that he had suffered a heart attack.

Roger eyed him curiously. Certainly Ned was very sombre.

"What is the prognosis, Ned?" He heard his own voice, but faint and far away. "Facts, please, Ned."

"Not good, I'm afraid."

"How long?"

"There's no time given, Roger."

"But time enough to make a new will, is that it?"

Ned looked pained but still resolute. "I think you'd be more at peace with yourself."

"Good old Ned, you never give up, do you? But you'll be glad to know that I don't have to make a new will. For I haven't got one. I tore up the last one because I had some new ideas about setting up the museum that I wanted to think over. If I died now, Osgood would get everything."

"Except for Kitty's dower rights."

"She waived them when I gave her the New York house."

Ned sat slowly down on the bed. He seemed suddenly very moved. "Roger, my dear brother, it's not just Osgood and the place I'm thinking of. It's you. Believe me. If you could just allow the normal succession of things in Castledale, you might rid yourself of the hate that's been eating away at your heart all these years."

"Hate? What are you talking about? Hatred of what?"

"I've never been sure. All I know is it's there. And that it's

always been there. At least ever since I can remember. Of
course, I'm seven years younger than you. Did it all start with
that duel?"

Roger stared with a new interest at this suddenly penetrating sibling. But he didn't answer the question. "I don't hate
you, Ned."

"I don't believe you do. But I'm part of Castledale. And
you certainly don't hate Castledale."

"But its ghosts hate me!"

"Maybe you could change that."

Roger considered this. "But if I give up this hate or obsession or whatever it is, won't it be too late? If I've lived with it
so long, what will I have in its place? For whatever time I may
have left?"

Ned actually shrugged. "Nothing in particular, I guess.
What I have. What other people have. Wouldn't that be
better?"

"Would Osgood and Felicia live here if the place was theirs?
How would they keep it up?"

"They'd have me to help them."

And Roger realized that, of course, Ned had been writing
to them. Well, why not? He closed his eyes as he felt the
emptiness coming over him again. If it should be another
attack, he could surrender to the soothing notion that he now
needn't do anything about anything. There was a wonderful
ease to Ned's concept of "nothing in particular." The pavilions
of the Lawn stretched down the valley of his mind to the great
dome with all the grace and tranquillity of Mr. Jefferson's
noble scheme. He could forget the fire and the sword and the
long sordid aftermath and soothe his tired spirits with the
blessed memory of the red dirt and blue hills beyond a serene
Castledale.

HERMES

God of the Self-Made Man

MY FATHER changed his name from Oscar Ullman to Oscar Leonard in 1885, only a year before he changed (in wedlock) my mother's from Hettie Straus to Hettie Leonard. To him it was neither an important nor a particularly significant act; it was his simple assertion to the world that he refused to be identified too obviously with a particular race or religion. "Leonard," he would say, "commits me to nothing — I can be a citizen of the globe." But to his and Mother's New York relatives, including such distinguished interrelated families of German-Jewish origin as Seligmans, Lewisohns and Lehmans, though few of them had retained the Orthodox faith, his gesture, while not ranked as outright treachery, was sneered at as unworthy of a gentleman, as the repudiation of a noble heritage and, even worse, as a truckling to the Protestant establishment. They continued to receive my parents — indeed, their sympathy for the cousin now referred to as "poor, bullied Hettie" would alone have guaranteed that — but whenever introductions at a party were needed, you would be sure to hear: "And this is my cousin Oscar Ullman — oh, I *beg* your pardon — what am I thinking of — Oscar *Leonard*, of course."

Father didn't mind. I sometimes thought he didn't mind anything. He was a big, breezy, broad-chested man with high, wavy, once prematurely grey hair and a loud resonant voice. He had achieved some degree of fame as a popular professor of philosophy at Columbia and had written a couple of best sellers: *The Wish for the Deed* and *My Brother's Keeper*. He was forceful and fearless, with a great capacity for enjoying life, which his modest share of a much-divided family fortune enabled him sufficiently to implement. Mother was very dear and very loving, but with little of his powerful intellect; she acted as his pleasant but by no means uncritical helpmate, showing at all times a remarkable equanimity of temper, but I suspect that she harbored inner doubts as to the wisdom or even the ethics of his having distanced himself from the tribe. The inspiration and education of their only child fell inevitably upon her mate.

Father was determined that I should grow up as free a soul as he. "The world can be your oyster, my boy," he used to tell me, "if you only have the guts to swallow it." But it was the world of the spirit that he meant. Father loved good food and good wine and shiny gadgets and machines — he was an early convert to the automobile and tore about the dirt roads of Westchester with goggles in an open Bentley — but he had no interest in social or worldly success and tried to impress upon me that the only use of any money that he should give or leave me was to render me free to observe and think and perhaps create. He constantly mocked the materialism of our much richer relatives, I think because he suspected that my genes contained a goodly share of it. And of course he was

right. I was greedier than even he divined. I wanted everything. I wanted their world as well as his.

I also wanted to go to a New England boarding school, for
I had learned that their graduates enjoyed a preferred social
status at Yale and Harvard. Some of these academies, by no
means all, accepted Jewish boys, but Father wouldn't hear of
it. He didn't want me to encounter anti-Semitism in any form
until I was old enough and tough enough to put it in what he
at least considered its proper perspective. He had very definite
ideas on the subject, which he set forth later in his privately
printed memoirs:

"Anti-Semitism in Europe, having its roots in the Dark
Ages when a united Catholic Church portrayed Jews as the
crucifiers of their god, was a vicious and almost unbeatable
superstition. But in the USA, where religion has played only
a minor role and where no federal or state government can
enforce or even recognize it, weak little creeds multiply like
thistles. There is thus no prevailing orthodoxy that can be
martialed against Jews whose unpopularity may be attributed
only to their greater success in the marketplace. Rich or even
well-to-do Gentiles, therefore, have no cause to be jealous of
Jews, and such anti-Semitism as exists in their ranks is a kind
of inherited convention or even mannerism that has no real
basis and will be put aside any time they find it convenient to
develop a relationship with a particular Jew. Indeed, it will
often become clear that they do not know what a Jew is,
though a not inconsiderable number of them have some strain
of Hebraic ancestry."

I attended a private day school on the west side of Central
Park where at least half the boys were Jewish, as were a good
proportion of the family friends who came to our parties at the
big sunny apartment on Riverside Drive or the grey stone villa

in Rye, so that when I went to Yale in 1907 I had not
encountered any social milieu where I was not deemed as good
as anyone else. Indeed, as I led my class in scholastic achieve-
ment and as my burly figure was an asset on the athletic field,
I was inclined to feel myself a superior being. But I was not
my father's pupil for nothing. I never lost sight of a world in
which I might have to start at a disadvantage. He had taught
me, above anything else, even things of the spirit, to be a
realist.

At Yale that world indeed revealed itself, but for the first
two years I was too proud — and too cautious — to expose
myself to its sting. I worked hard for the high marks that I
continued to obtain and confined myself largely to the company of those friends from my New York academy who had
gone with me to New Haven. But I noted everything that
went on on that campus, how men dressed and talked, what
fraternities and societies were the most cultivated, what careers
were looked forward to. And I think what most prompted me
at last to seek to enlarge my social scope was the remark of a
Harvard professor of philosophy, a superb old Boston snob,
whose passion for the subject he taught had prevailed over his
prejudice to induce him to visit my parents in Rye. When I
told him, in response to his polite but perfunctory inquiries as
to how I spent my time in New Haven, that I largely studied,
he replied with a nod: "So wise of you. If you had cared for
undergraduate frolics, you had done better with us. No Yale
man, you know, is ever quite a gentleman."

Now the odd thing about this fatuous remark was that I
thought I could see some truth in it. I *had* observed that there
was a rackety, "boola-boola," not so disarmingly boyish aspect
to even the elite of my class that contrasted unfavorably with
the more languid, more disdainful airs of the sons of Brahmins
whom I had observed on a visit to Harvard Yard. Of course,

it was all nonsense. But it was a nonsense with which I was beginning to see it should not be insuperably difficult for me to cope.

My first step in junior year was to elect William Lyon (Billy) Phelps's course in British nineteenth-century poets, with its heavy, its almost exclusive emphasis on Robert Browning. All the golden youth flocked to this. I had my eye in particular on two first cousins who were also roommates in Vanderbilt Hall: Gurdon and Horace Aspinwall. They came of an old Manhattan clan; they had gone to Groton School in Massachusetts, and they knew everyone in the group on which I had fixed my eye. Gurdon, I had heard, was supposed to be "snotty," but Horace had a reputation of amiability, and when I took a seat by him in class he responded affably to my overtures.

"Do you really like Browning?" I asked, as we crossed the old campus after class.

"Of course! Isn't he the greatest of the great?"

"Which of his poems do you prefer?"

"Oh, the love ones, don't you? 'Evelyn Hope' and 'The Last Ride Together.' "

"But are they really love poems? Aren't they too unilateral? Evelyn Hope is only a dead little girl. And the reason it's the last ride is that he's been turned down."

"But that's just my trouble, you see," he admitted with a grin that was half sheepish, half almost proud. "Unrequited love." He paused to sigh. "I trust that won't happen to you. Which poems do you prefer?"

I had to think. "I suppose the Renaissance ones. Those about coldhearted villainous Italian nobles. Like the murderous duke in 'My Last Duchess.' Or Guido in *The Ring and the Book*. I feel they're the real Browning."

"You mean he *wanted* to be like that?"

"He wanted power. Like so many artists. And they know they're never going to get it. So they enjoy fantasizing about it." I shrugged. "Maybe I say that only because *I* do."

"That's very interesting. Why don't we have lunch and discuss it? Come to my frat."

I accepted. I knew he belonged to Psi U. I think he would have said "fraternity" to one of his Groton friends. But as so frequently happens in college life, a friendship was established that same day. I found myself a welcome visitor in the rooms he shared with his cousin Gurdon.

Horace was much handsomer than Gurdon, though I don't know why I say that, because Gurdon wasn't really handsome at all, despite a balding, gleaming, eye-snapping, big-nosed desire to appear so. Perhaps it was because you didn't realize that Horace *was* handsome until you compared him with someone else. His figure was lithe and well knit, but there was just a suggestion of slightness to it. His auburn hair was thick and long with a mild wave, and in profile his pallor and Greek nose gave him something of the air of a poet, but his determined stride across the campus in the company of his peers suggested a half-defiant need to proclaim himself "one of the boys." In the same way his wide brown eyes, after fixing you with a luminous and faintly distrustful stare, would suddenly flash in mockery, and you would hear his cheerful but rather coarse laugh. But he willed the coarseness; that was the point. He could be very funny indeed, but he could also be very serious, and the latter mood, I soon learned, was the truer one. Horace was never sure of himself, but he had from childhood, I suspected, been very sure that he had to be a good boy.

Young men, as I have implied, become intimate easily, and Horace and I were no exceptions. He never showed the slight-

est awareness of the difference in our backgrounds; he had
been born, so far as I could make out, without a snobbish
bone in his body. It was true that his friends, except for me,
were all drawn from the same milieu, but that was because
this milieu had been his natural habitat. That he had not had
the imagination or even the curiosity to change it might have
been simply the result of his failure to see that other habitats
were any different.

Gurdon was much more sophisticated, a natural snob born
with the wit to conceal it. He was very social, an accomplished
manipulator of men, smart and shrewd, with eyes that sparkled with the intent to convey an air of friendly mischief and
a braying, humorless laugh. He treated Horace more like a
kid brother than a cousin of equal age, and I had little doubt
that he regarded me with a distinct suspicion, as if he could
not believe that a man as intelligent as I obviously was would
be cultivating Horace from motives of simple friendship. But
he was cordial enough. Gurdon would never discard a card
until he was sure it had no value. Not unlike myself.

It was probably because of Gurdon's superiority in worldly
wisdom that Horace found me a more comfortable confidant
to hear of his love for Dorothy Stonor. She was the only child
of the second marriage of the twice-widowered Frank Stonor,
with whose famous career I was sufficiently familiar, the
streetcar magnate and statesman who had served briefly in
Cleveland's cabinet and was known as the patrician liberal who
had reared a sober brownstone cube on a prominent corner of
Fifth Avenue to mock the garish derivative palaces of his
nouveaux riches neighbors. The snapshot of his beloved that
Horace carried in his wallet showed me a handsome rather
than pretty girl with straight dark hair tied at the back of her
neck, a firm nose and chin and candid, inquiring eyes. You

could see that she was honest and would be frank. Perhaps even too much so.

"Why do you think it's all so hopeless?" I asked. "Aren't you considered rather a catch? By mothers in Gotham, any-way?"

"But Dorothy doesn't have a mother. Hers died when she was a baby."

"Well, by fathers, then."

"Oh, Mr. Stonor has no use for the likes of me. How could he? A poor college student with law school still ahead of him."

"But surely your family has money."

"Not what he calls money. Dorothy will have *millions*, Maury."

"I don't see that as a drawback. Besides, I thought these tycoons liked to marry their daughters into old families."

"But Mr. Stonor comes of an old family himself! The only thing self-made about him is his fortune. No, he has very different plans for his princess."

"Such as a foreign title?"

"They're out of fashion now." Horace pondered for a minute and then admitted, "I guess I don't really know what he wants except that it's sure as hell something a lot better than Horace Aspinwall."

"But can't Dorothy decide for herself? Or are we still in the day of arranged marriages?"

"No, no, Dorothy could never be forced into anything. But she's terribly under her father's influence. She was brought up as an only child by one parent. Her half-brothers are much older and long married. She considers Daddy a kind of god."

"And how does she feel about you?"

"Oh, she likes me well enough. She always seems glad to see me, and she writes me when she goes off on trips with her old man. In fact she's too nice to me; that's one of my troubles. She treats me more as a pal than a beau."

"But she must know how you really feel?"

"Oh, yes!" Horace's face lit up with his sense of this. But at once it seemed to drop. "Only she brushes it off. She mutters about our being too young and not knowing our own minds — things her father has told her, no doubt."

"Puppy love?" I was sorry for the term when I saw the pain in his eyes.

"I daresay Mr. Stonor *would* call it that."

My parents were in England; Father was teaching for a term at Oxford, and Horace invited me for a weekend at his parents' house in New York. It was to be the occasion of my meeting the famous Dorothy. But first let me say something about his family.

They were certainly not rich by the standards of 1909; their brownstone with a stoop on East Fifty-sixth Street had only a three-window frontage, and a picture in the hall of their summer cottage in Maine showed an unpretentious shingle pile. But they kept five maids and hired a motor when needed, and Horace's father belonged to several clubs to which he rarely went. The interior of the brownstone, virgin to the reforming hands of Elsie de Wolfe and Elizabeth Marbury, was conventionally cluttered, though relics of the Federal period, mute emblems of the finer taste and greater affluence of an earlier generation, peeped out between trinket-filled *étagères* and bronze groups of animals in alarming combat. I recall in particular a lovely Aspinwall bride in marble, done in Rome on an 1840 honeymoon, and the miniature of a romantic youth with a grace and charm not unlike Horace's.

Mrs. Aspinwall was a small reserved woman, with lips that seemed always pursed and an air of mild benevolence ever ready to be withdrawn, who cosseted a supposedly frail health. I say "supposedly," though certainly none of her family ever doubted its frailty. Her confidence that the duties from which her weakened state exempted her would be performed by her husband and children was entirely justified in the fact.

Her husband was a large man with a larger stomach who might have been handsome enough as a youth, but who was now the product of physical inactivity (except for fishing), much eating and (I suspect) private drinking in the study where he spent most of his day. He had no occupation when I knew him except handling his and his wife's securities, though he had once served on a couple of railroad boards and even, according to a family legend, been kicked off that of Illinois Central for opposing Mr. Harriman. This was always cited by his children as an example of his courage and independence, but Gurdon, who saw his uncle with a less partial eye, told me that it had been simply a case of Uncle John's awakening from his usual snoozle at a directors' meeting and forgetting for once his role of rubber stamp.

Both he and his wife carried self-absorption to a high degree, but whereas she could at least turn her attention to a guest on a social occasion, he was almost incapable of taking in anything you tried to tell him and would fix a glassy eye on you until he had a chance (soon seized if not offered) to put in a story of his fishing or stock market acumen (the latter, again according to Gurdon, a total fiction). So removed was he from any sense of what people might notice that he must have believed that his noisy habit of scraping his molars with a toothpick behind his napkin went unobserved. Gurdon at Yale used to embarrass Horace by "doing Uncle John" for an irreverent group, throwing a towel over his face and making rasping sounds from behind it. But Mr. Aspinwall's indifference to the world was interpreted in his family as gentle kindliness and his platitudes as the tip of a concealed iceberg of wisdom.

Horace's two younger sisters, Chattie and Lizzie, were much alike, plain and bumptious, prone to ecstatic enthusiasms and sudden storms of tears, and given at table to high screeches of laughter after whispered confidences soon subdued by a glance from their rarely amused mother. They had kind hearts, however, and the warmth of their sympathy supplied the sex appeal with which they both ultimately obtained surprisingly attractive husbands.

Stewart, the eldest, aspired to be the dapper dandy of the day. He was always immaculately and colorfully dressed, but saved from foppishness at a rather high cost by the rigidity of his stature, the length of his nose and the cold stare of his grey eyes. He resembled his younger cousin Gurdon, but had few of his brains. He loved to play the man of the world, the showy soul of courtesy in the drawing room to the ladies, but always ready with a sly poke in my ribs to assure me that he was equally welcome in very different female company. His mother unaccountably adored him, almost to the exclusion of her other children.

How could she fail to see that Horace was the star of the family? But she did fail. And so did the others. Oh, the girls were fond enough of him in their demonstrative way; they responded to his good looks and shrieked at his jokes; Stewart found him a gratifying confidant for his amorous adventures; and even Mr. Aspinwall preferred him to the others as a fishing companion. But they couldn't, any of them, see that he was as strange an occupant of their noisy nest as if the egg from which he hatched had been deposited there by some irresponsible cuckoo bird. And with his mother I suspect it was something worse. I think she may have understood that Horace, for all his ostensible consideration of her aches and pains, had penetrated to the root of her inveterate selfishness. She may even have disliked him. For she made one flat statement to me: "Horry has shown me less affection than any of my other children. I wonder whether his isn't a cold nature."

She should have known!

Dorothy came to dinner on the Saturday night of my week-end visit. It was a tense occasion for Horace, as it was the first time she had met his parents, and I think he had waited for my moral support. She was very much what I had imagined: the serious, direct young lady of the era, determined not to be taken in by the "gold sachet" of its opulence and to find a life of civic usefulness compatible with a woman's domestic role. Looking back, I can see how little progress these brave young society women had really made; they were basically already mortgaged to their parents' standards. But though lacking any kind of subtle female charm, Dorothy was fresh and healthy and . . . well, I guess the adjective is "good." I have already used it about Horace. I could see perfectly why he was in love with her.

He wanted Dorothy and me to have a chance to chat alone, so he led us to a corner of the parlor where we waited for his mother to come down.

"Will you be going to law school, too, Mr. Leonard?" she asked me. I nodded. "I'm sure it's a fine career for a man."

"You sound as if you weren't entirely sure."

She was surprised to be so promptly taken up. "Well, my father always says he'd rather be a client."

"I suppose he hires lawyers by the dozen. He says to this one 'Come' and he cometh, and to that one 'Go' and he goeth."

"Now you're laughing at me, Mr. Leonard."

"Not at all. For I quite see his point. Why not be the boss

while you're at it? But what I like about the idea of being a lawyer, particularly a lawyer for businessmen and bankers, is that you're always dealing with the basic underpinnings of organized society. You can think and philosophize while you're making money. Most men act in a naturalistic play. I want mine to be in blank verse."

Of course I was playing with her. She stared at me suspiciously.

"My father doesn't act in a naturalistic play. Do you mean something like Ibsen? My father is very much concerned with history and philosophy. He's a great reader. And it may interest you to know that he's a friend of Mr. Adams, the historian, in Washington, and Mr. Adams sees only a small number of intellectual men."

"Oh, I know that," I responded airily. "Billy Phelps at Yale let me read his copy of *The Education of Henry Adams.* It's been privately printed. He mentions your father, you know. He says that like John Hay and Whitelaw Reid he owed his 'free hand' to marriage."

Dorothy's countenance lengthened ominously. "And just what does that imply, Mr. Leonard?"

"I assume it means that all three men married money. Wasn't that the case?"

Her gaze turned to Horace across the room with his sisters. "I think I had better join the others." She rose, but paused when I jumped up to protest.

"You disappoint me, Miss Stonor. I thought you were a modern woman."

"And should a modern woman sit by while her father is traduced?"

"Do you call being mentioned by our greatest historian a traducement?"

She resumed her seat at this, troubled. "I haven't read Mr. Adams's book. I know he sent Daddy a copy."

"Would he have sent it if it contained offensive matter?"

"No, I suppose not. And I suppose there are things a historian can mention that would not be proper on social occasions."

"And are you and I to be confined to what is said or not said on social occasions?"

She gave me a clear look. "All right, no, Mr. Leonard. But I want you to know that my father has made on his own a much larger fortune than what his first wife brought him."

I felt elated. I had made her break a tabu! She was actually talking about money. I was going on to point out that her father had at least got his start with his first wife's money, but I decided that would be pressing her too far.

"It can't be easy, being the daughter of such a famous man," I said, in a more conciliatory tone. "Horace says you've never shown the tiniest bit of vanity about it."

"Oh, Horace is too kind about me altogether." She laughed now, almost relaxed. "But you're right that it's not always easy. I remember, when I was in my last year at Miss Chapin's School, one of President Roosevelt's nieces or cousins, I forget which, said right out in class that Uncle Thee had called my father 'a malefactor of great wealth.' "

"I trust you didn't take *that* lying down."

"You can be sure I did not, Mr. Leonard!" Her eyes shone becomingly. "I retorted that my father had described the president as 'an irresponsible demagogue.' But, oh, I hated it!"

Mrs. Aspinwall now made her belated entrance with her usual air of having had to use a goodly portion of her store of courage to rise from a bed of pain. In the dining room the conversation, marred by an occasional explosion of giggles from Horace's sisters and his father's veiled teeth cleansing, was led by his mother. She asked a few quiet, banal questions about a course in literature that Dorothy was auditing at Columbia.

"I suppose you read all the great classics, Cooper and Hawthorne and Mrs. Stowe."

"Oh, yes, we read them," Dorothy confirmed. "But the course takes us right up to date also. We have read Howells and Henry James. And next week we're going to discuss Mrs. Wharton's *House of Mirth*."

"Edith Wharton? You surprise me, Miss Stonor. I shouldn't have thought her work would be considered in a serious course of American letters."

"You don't like her books?"

"I don't say they're not entertaining. But they are full of society gossip. I used to know her in Newport when she was Miss Jones. Pussie, she was called then. Her parents were friends of my parents, but she gave herself airs. I think she considered that she was too intellectual for Newport. We were only good enough, I suppose, to be made fun of in her fiction. Well, now, it seems that our Pussie has matured into a full-grown cat."

This was an unusual exercise in wit for Mrs. Aspinwall, and she looked down the table with a mild gratification as all but Dorothy laughed.

"My father admires Mrs. Wharton," the latter observed, as if this should lead to a general retraction.

"Well, your father always had rather advanced ideas. In my opinion they sit better with gentlemen than with ladies."

"Oh, do you know my father, Mrs. Aspinwall?" Dorothy asked with a surprise that she did not appear to consider might be rude.

"I *did* know him, certainly. Again in Newport, in our younger days. It was a smaller society then. You might say that everybody knew everybody. My father used to say of your father: 'Watch that young man. He's going to make his mark.' "

The extraordinary thing about Horace's mother was the way she could make her judgments appear absolute. Even Dorothy seemed to react as if Mr. Stonor had received some kind of ultimate accolade. What was it to have made a fortune or even sat in the cabinet of President Cleveland (a Democrat, after all) compared with the distinction of having attracted the notice of an old Newporter like Beverly Beekman on a summer day in 1880?

Horace seemed very pleased at Dorothy's reception by his family. I believe that he accepted as praise from the heart the perfunctory approval of the evening that she may have conceded to him in the cab when he took her home. The sainted Dorothy could speak nothing but the truth, could she? At any rate when he came back and after we had retired to his bedroom, which we shared, he kept me up half the night singing the praises of his "wonderful girl." He also professed great gratification at the impression I had apparently made on her.

"She said she was glad I at last had an interesting friend and not just another New England church school type."

Horace had charm, but he could be a bore. I suppose most people in love can be.

I returned to New Haven that Sunday morning, as I had a paper to prepare for a Monday class, but Horace stayed on to lunch at the Stonors' and escort Dorothy in the afternoon to an exhibit of miniatures at the Metropolitan Museum. He would take a late afternoon train back and said he would drop by my room in the evening. But nothing in his plan prepared me for the pale face and reddened eyes that confronted me when I answered a late knock on my door.

"It's all over!" he exclaimed dramatically and stumbled past me to slump on my sofa.

"What's all over?"

"Me and Dorothy. Or rather me."

He sat up suddenly straight now, holding himself very still, as if the least movement might cause a twinge of pain.

"I take it then she's sent you packing."

"Well, not quite. She says we can still be friends."

"That's the usual way, isn't it?"

At this he began actually to sob, and I turned away in embarrassment.

"I'm sorry, Maury." He wiped his eyes. "I'll try not to be such an ass. She sprang it on me in the museum, right in front of that Sargent painting of the three sisters in white. She's going abroad with her father for three months."

"Is that against the law?"

"But they're going to meet that oily protégé of her father's, Guy Thorp, in Marseille! He's going to join them for a Mediterranean cruise on a yacht Mr. Stonor has chartered. I told her she'd meet all kinds of dukes and princes and never give another thought to Horace Aspinwall!"

He looked more fourteen than twenty as he said this.

"And what did she say to *that?*" I asked roughly. "That she never would? If she did, you deserved it."

"No! She said she'd always value my friendship. But she got furious when I told her she'd probably come back engaged to Thorp."

"I don't wonder. It'll be your own fault if she does."

He looked aghast. "How will I have done that?"

"By whimpering. By playing the little boy who doesn't dare

so much as touch his goddess's fingertips. What woman wants to be treated that way? Except perhaps some frigid old maid, which your Dorothy is very far from being."

"Just as far as she is from being *my* Dorothy. No, Maury, it won't do. I'm not in her league, any way you look at it. I've given her up, and I've written her so. And don't try to talk me out of it, because I know it's the best thing for both of us."

Well, of course, I wasn't going to let that pass, and we sat up a large part of the night arguing. By early morning I had induced him at least to reconsider, and I sent him off to bed with the assurance that we would discuss a plan of action the following afternoon.

But that next morning, when I had returned to my room from a nine o'clock class, I received my first visit there from Horace's cousin. Gurdon entered when I answered his knock with his usual twinkling condescension.

"I trust I'm not intruding?" When I assured him he was not, he came in and looked around at his ease. "But you have made yourself very comfortable, I see. Much more elegant than anything we have at poor old Vanderbilt. What nice things you've got! May I inquire who is the lovely young lady? A very particular friend, I hope?"

"It's a pencil sketch of my mother as a girl. By Millais."

"Oh, I see. Very fine indeed." He continued to allow his appraising eye to roam. At last he took a seat and cleared his throat. But still no word.

"Gurdon, is there something on your mind?"

"In fact there is. You won't object if I'm frank?"

"Not if you really are."

"You don't trust me, do you, Maury? You haven't from the beginning."

"I simply like to know where I stand."

"Then here it is. Horace told me this morning that he had made up his mind to give up his romance with Dorothy Stonor — if that's the right word for an affair so one-sided — but that you, it appears, have persuaded him to go on with it."

"Is that so wrong?"

"We are a proud family, Maurice. You come of one yourself, so you know whereof I speak. It has never been our way to push in where we are not wanted."

"Not wanted by whom? By Dorothy or her father?"

"By both, I'm afraid. Mr. Stonor's candidate for his daughter's hand is obviously Guy Thorp. Do you know about Guy Thorp?"

"Horace has mentioned him."

"He's worth more than a mention. He's a very courtly diplomat, currently attached to our embassy in London. Considered brilliant. Some thirty years of age, of no particular fortune, but backed by the mighty Stonor, who presumably intends to make an ambassador of him. Or maybe even one day a secretary of state. Who knows, in these days of fat campaign funds?"

"And how does Dorothy feel about this paragon?"

"I think the best way to put that might be that she feels he's inevitable."

"You mean she *has* to have him? But why, in God's name?"

"Because he's so damned appropriate. Because he's what Doctor Daddy has ordered. Because she feels that a dutiful daughter should have a very good reason indeed before turning down so fine and upstanding a suitor. And I very much doubt whether she will see our Horace as such a reason."

I saw, of course, that Gurdon, in Mr. Stonor's place, would have behaved in just the same way. I understood perfectly that

Gurdon was the prototype of the grinning imp who would always be poor Horace's worst enemy.

"Let us suppose, Gurdon, that everything you say is true. What does Horace have to lose by fighting for something he so desperately wants?"

"His self-respect. Horace is a very delicate instrument, more so than you can probably imagine. He is very good at concealing his vulnerability. But in the family, we know. He is subject to dangerous spells of depression. In our sixth-form year at Groton, for example, when he failed to make the varsity football team his spirits were so low that I had to write Aunt Lydia and Uncle John to take him out of school. He was gone for two whole months."

"I see." Horace had told me something about this, but not of the length of the absence. "But if Horace is going to duck every challenge in life because it may bring on a depression, where is he going to get?"

"I never said he should duck *every* challenge. You may not trust me, Maurice, but even you will have to ask, where Horace is concerned, what motive could possibly guide me but his welfare."

I knew well enough how I *could* have answered his question: "The desire to keep someone whom you have always sought to dominate from becoming a bigger and richer man than yourself!"

But of course I said no such thing. How would that have helped Horace? I simply suggested that we should have to agree to disagree and regretted that I had to leave him to finish my term paper in the library.

Horace's resolution not to relinquish his pursuit of Dorothy could be implemented only by correspondence in the next three months. His particular concern was with Thorp.

"What chance do I have against a guy who's already on the spot?" he asked me gloomily.

"The chance of being able to show only your best side in your letters. Thorp may make an ass of himself, who knows? Anything can happen on that boat. And if she chances to feel a bit pushed around by Daddy and a bit taken for granted by his too-obvious candidate, a breezy cheerful letter from you may hit just the right note. The great thing is not to be mawkish. Make her wonder whether you may not be turning into a bigger person without her."

What is rarer than a friend who takes one's advice? Horace went back to his room and wrote out a long letter, which he then asked me to read. But I declined.

"You must get out of the habit of seeking people's approval." I was thinking of Gurdon. "You don't need it."

He became thoughtful at this, and after a minute he asked, "If I should propose to do something nice for you, Maury, would you put it down to my seeking your approval?"

"Not if it was nice enough. What are you proposing? I warn you in advance that I'll accept it."

"Don't be too hasty. I want you to think it over first. I'd like to put you up for Psi U."

I whistled. Then I tried to pass it off with a pun. "The first Jew in Psi U? It even rhymes."

"There's got to be a first time for everything."

"Horry, whom are you trying to kid? You know you'd never get me in."

"Don't be too sure. You're giving me a new confidence in myself. Well, let's see how it goes."

As I studied his countenance I thought I could indeed make out a new confidence. At the same time it occurred to me that perhaps I should let him do what he proposed, as much for his sake as for my own. More, really, for a fraternity as "chic" as his would be socially a seven-league-boot stride that could hurt me as much as it helped in the antagonisms it might create.

At any rate, after some days' rumination, I agreed to be put up, and Horace at once went to work. He arranged to have me seconded by the member of his Groton group whom I most liked, Ethan Barlow, and this did much to reconcile me to the tussle that was bound to follow. Barlow was, like me, a robust fellow with thick curly black hair, but unlike me he had a distinctly patrician air. He was a first-class athlete with a first-class (though not original) mind, and a natural leader in our Yale class, softening the impression of his sometimes exhausting energy with the warmth of his natural charm. When he grabbed you by the elbow and suggested a Saturday excursion to New York following a six-mile morning run to take in a matinée of Nazimova in Ibsen and an evening on the town, you threw down your books and went along. It might go without saying that he worshipped Theodore Roosevelt and lamented that he had been born too late to have been a Rough Rider.

I knew that my father would disapprove of the fraternity business, as indeed he did, answering my letter with three sentences: "I should never have abandoned one chaining tradition to be shackled to another. But who knows? *You* may find it at least amusing." What I did find amusing, or at least interesting, was that Horace, in promoting me, showed a good deal more political shrewdness than I had imagined him to possess. He played skillfully on his friends' desire not to appear stuffy and went so far as to suggest that the fraternity would get the credit for admitting a Jew who wasn't really a Jew at all, thus having and eating its cake of broad-mindedness. When I learned of this from the candid Ethan Barlow, I put it to him that my honor might require me to withdraw my name.

"But you can't do that to Horry after all his work! It wouldn't be like you, Maury. I thought you were out to conquer the world."

"Only if it's worth conquering."

"And I've been thinking of you as a kind of Genghis Khan!"

"Would he have joined Psi U?"

"If only to turn it into a pile of skulls."

Well, of course, he was right: I couldn't do that to Horace, and I accepted my hard-earned election. Looking back, I must admit that the fraternity afforded me much pleasure. My memory of the old campus with its frame of dark, homely buildings is permeated with an atmosphere of noisy enthusiasm, of amiable brainlessness, of ingenuous idealism. There were members of Psi U it was impossible not to like, and I thought I preferred one Eli to a dozen Harvard "gentlemen." But at the time I had another reservation, which I also put to Ethan.

"I don't mind owing an election to you and Horace. But I must admit I'd hate to owe it to Gurdon."

Ethan looked at me sharply. "Why so?"

"Because he doesn't like me. Oh, it's not that he's not pleasant enough. But I get the distinct feeling that he thinks his cousin stepped rather far off the reservation in making such a pal of me."

Ethan considered his answer to this for a few moments. "I may be out of order, but if thinking you owe Gurdon anything is going to spoil the idea of Psi U for you, I'd better speak out. Gurdon hasn't helped your candidacy a bit. In fact, he opposed it. When Horry wasn't around to hear him, he actually talked you down."

I think this information did more than anything else to make me appreciate my election. If the issue was important enough to make Gurdon disloyal to his cousin and roommate, the fraternity might have more than a mere undergraduate importance in life.

"Do me a favor, Ethan. Promise me you'll never tell Gurdon that you've told me."

"But I had every intention of doing so! I'd feel like a sneak otherwise."

"Feel like a sneak then. Please. How could I ever feel easy in his and Horace's rooms if he knew that I knew?"

Ethan agreed to be silent, though he may have suspected that I had not given him my real reason. I suspected even then that Gurdon was destined to cut a bigger figure in the world than his cousin, and I had no wish to throw away any potential asset, certainly not for the petty satisfaction of showing a mean man that I knew of his meanness.

My election to Psi U, however, resulted also in a pleasanter discovery: the charmingly tactful side of Horace's nature. I wanted to acknowledge his sponsorship with an appropriate gesture, and I ordered from Tiffany's a gold tie pin with a sapphire over our intertwined initials. He showed an enthusiastic gratitude, wore it once on a New York weekend and then put it away, saying it was too fine for any but the grandest occasions. Of course I never saw it again, and it did not take me long to realize that this florid piece with its sentimental expression of friendship had been in the worst possible taste. I winced as I imagined Gurdon drawling, "They just never learn, do they?" But then I recognized that Horace would never have shown it to Gurdon. He would have understood how quickly one as observant as I *would* learn, and he was much too considerate to assail me with a lecture on breeding that could not have seemed anything but condescending. Which is one reason that Horace has been one of the few people in my life I have loved.

The elation that Horace felt with Dorothy's warmer answers to his letters was, in my opinion, an exaggerated reaction even to the affection that he read into them. But it showed how repressed he had been. He put me in mind of a handsome painted puppet released from his strings and cavorting about the stage on his own. It may have seemed to him that he had spent his life adjusting himself to the role in which he deemed his family to have cast him: the freckled kid in knickers, with hair either too slickly brushed or hopelessly messy, whom his elders liked smilingly to call "incorrigible," but whose harmless mischievousness and sound healthy appetites could be counted on to guard him from the vices that peculiarly infected an American Eden.

He may even have apprehended that only by preserving such an image could he be forgiven the good looks and boyish charm that his mother seemed almost to deprecate, as if he had manifested a kind of hubris in offering so unflattering a contrast to his fatuous older brother and his squealing sisters. For if his family depended on him, so to speak, to reconcile them with the brownstone community of Manhattan, if without him to dress up the background his father might have seemed a pompous nincompoop and his mother a complaining valetudinarian, it was in no way to Horace's credit, but simply the evidence of a duty imposed on him by an arcane power which would promptly expose him as the lowest of frauds should he forget for a minute the lines of his given part.

I can go even further, now that I am launched in Freudian reminiscence. I venture to perceive in the very arrangement of the floors of the Aspinwalls' brownstone the scaffold that upheld and supported Horace's neurosis. Such small distinction as this edifice could boast diminished as you rose on the high straight stairs, and when you reached the fourth floor with Horace's and his sisters' rooms (the five maids huddled in cubicles above), you were faced with the plainest of brown wood factory-made furniture and walls adorned with cheap prints of academic paintings. What, however, particularly marked the junior status of this level was that whereas on the floor below each of Horace's parents and their older son enjoyed a separate bathroom, the fourth story was equipped with but a single water closet, though its availability for all of the younger Aspinwalls seemed curiously indicated by its possession of three doors. It was the modest, even the prudish habit of Horace's sisters to lock all three portals when they were using the plumbing, but when they exited they would invariably unlatch only one. Horace therefore might have to try two doors unsuccessfully before gaining access, and when either Chattie or Lizzie was actually within she would never give him warning by singing out "Someone's in here!" but wait until he had assailed the locked third and then shout a triumphant, "Yenh, yenh!"

It may sound fanciful, but I suggest that Horace's association of himself with the two female co-tenants of the water closet had some relation to his earlier sense of unworthiness in respect to Dorothy. He may have come to regard that mocking cry from behind the trio of locked doors, followed soon by a vulgar cascade, as a brutal association of sex with excretion in which he and his silly sisters were irretrievably caught, whereas his father and brother below, real men, performing their natural functions in dignified and unintruded-upon silence, reserved their genital energy for females whom it could only awe.

Anyway, that family must have done *something* to him!

*   *   *

I speak with some inevitable hindsight when I describe the *dramatis personae* of my life, but I think it is true to say that from my first serious conversation with Frank Stonor I had spotted him as a man dominated by a single passion: the need to impress a world that he despised. Seated in a black carved Elizabethan armchair before a blazing fire in the immense log-walled hall of his Adirondacks "cabin," under the severed heads of bear, moose, and elk, the highest hanging thirty feet above him, his affectation of formal attire in the wilderness, even to a high collar and scarlet tie (though there might have been a small concession in the dark tweeds), seemed to pro-claim that a white-haired gentleman of such opaquely gazing eyes, of so high and brown a brow, with a gnarled hand so firmly grasping the gold head of a rarely relinquished cane, had needed nothing but his presence to smite fatally the beasts whose horns and tusks now harmlessly threatened him.

That he should spend his money in a forest where none but carefully selected guests, conveyed thither by a private rail-way, could see the results, rather than on a villa in Newport visible to other villas, was typical of his inverted snobbishness. I doubt that he feared anything on earth except that he might be taken as a fair representative of any group or class. In a Republican society, he was a politically active Democrat who delighted in alienating fellow tycoons by supporting (at least at the dinner table) government regulation of business. In a new plutocracy concerned with draping its genealogical nudity in purchased pedigrees, he liked to boast that the Stonors descended from sheep stealers in Norfolk and had bought their crest at Tiffany's. And confronted with the showy collections of old masters by means of which the financial leaders of the day hoped to hitch a ride to immortality, he would shrug and say that the souls of ancient commercial societies were best expressed in the beautiful gold coins that he displayed in glass cases in his office.

There was to be a house party of young people at his camp a couple of weeks after he and his daughter returned from Europe, and it was even rumored that it might be the occasion of the announcement of Dorothy's engagement to Guy Thorp. Horace was invited, and so, surprisingly, was I.

"I told you she liked you," Horace explained.

"Maybe she wants someone to catch you if you faint dead away at the news."

"Oh, Maury, is it possible? Can she really be going to marry that man? Why have you been urging me on so?"

But I was more irritated than touched by his woebegone look. How could a man care so much and have so little fight in him? I took from his hand the letter in which my invitation was included and read it.

"Well, at least she tells you just who's coming and when. Thorp isn't getting there until Monday, and we're asked for the preceding Friday. That gives you the whole weekend to make your play."

"Oh, she's just giving herself time to reconcile me to the news before the hero arrives."

"Fight, man, will you! Fight!"

And fight he actually did. For one whole day. When we arrived in the Adirondacks we were greeted by a Dorothy who was friendly but reserved. On Saturday morning she took Horace off on an all-day ride in the woods, leaving me behind with the other guests, none of whom I knew and none of whom showed the least interest in getting to know me. Mr. Stonor, however, proved unexpectedly cordial. It appeared that he had read and enjoyed my father's books, and he invited me to go fishing with him on the lake that afternoon in a large rowboat oared by a guide who sat near the bow. Mr. Stonor paid scant attention to the sport, letting the guide, as we drifted, do the casting for him and hand him the rod only on the rare occasions when a fish was hooked. I did my own casting, of course, but I paused whenever it looked as if Mr. Stonor wanted to talk. After all, I was there to be of assistance to Horace. When he embarked at last on a topic that seemed to interest him, I dropped my rod, lit a pipe and listened.

"You may have made the right decision to go into law, young man. Dorothy has described you as ambitious. When I was your age the future was all in business and banking. But now the railways are laid down, the frontier's gone and the oil wells are pumping. The captains and the kings have departed, and it's time for the little men to litigate over the spoils."

"I gather you don't think much of lawyers. Dorothy hinted as much."

"I don't think much of anybody, Leonard. I take the world as it comes. I was watching you at lunch, because of what Dorothy told me about you. You obviously didn't know any of her silly friends, but you held your own well enough. You strike me as a man who wants to run things rather than be run. In my day we old capitalists pretty much took the law into our own hands. But that day is over. In the future it's the lawyer who will tell us how to do what we want to do."

"How to get around the law, you mean, sir?"

Mr. Stonor shrugged. "If you want to put it that way. I look to acts, not definitions. Anyway, it's going to be a world that a clever lawyer should be able to dominate. Tell me, young man: Who in your opinion has been the most powerful American of the past decade?"

"Wouldn't that be President Roosevelt?"

"Well, he'd certainly like to think so. He told me once, as if it were something to the last degree presumptuous, that Pierpont Morgan, conferring with him in the White House, appeared to treat him as an equal. But I have no doubt that Morgan considered him an inferior. If you had seen as I did, last year in the panic, our financial leaders waiting respectfully outside the door of Morgan's great art-studded library to be admitted, one by one, each to submit his plan of how to save the nation to the silent figure bent over his game of solitaire, you would have witnessed a demonstration of real power. The great Theodore, for all his trumpeting, couldn't have done it. But it was nonetheless the end of an era."

"Horace's mother told me that her father had spotted you as a man who would make his mark in life when you were only my age. Is that what you are doing to me, sir? If so, I certainly appreciate it."

"Mrs. Aspinwall's father didn't have much else to choose from in the Newport of that day. Still, it was nice of her to say so. Little Lydia Beekman — I remember her well. Pretty as a picture. She was a friend of my younger sister's. But she threw herself away on John Aspinwall."

"They seemed compatible enough to me."

"Then he must have brought her down to his level. Men like that do."

And then we returned to our fishing. That evening before dinner Horace came to my room, where I was reading. There were actual tears in his eyes. "It's all over. The engagement will be announced on Thursday night."

"Can't you get her at least to put it off? A day's ride is hardly giving you a fair chance."

"Why should she give me any sort of chance?"

"Why has she been writing to you? Why has she been

stringing you along? Why did her father have to take her abroad to get her away from you? Hell's bells, man, you don't know your own power."

"But, Maury, it's just what I do know. And I suspect you do, too. It isn't decent for a man to hang on after he's been definitely rejected. I'm leaving the camp tonight. The little train is taking me out at six. Are you coming with me?"

I eyed him defiantly. "No!"

"What do you expect to accomplish here?"

"I don't know!"

He sighed. "There are times, Maury, when I can't help wondering if it was a good idea we ever met."

He left by the train as planned, and Dorothy seemed surprised, but not wholly displeased, that I did not accompany him.

Gurdon, I had later to admit, had been right about his cousin's nervous state of mind. Horace underwent a severe depression and had to leave Yale for six months while he retreated to a sanatorium, postponing his graduation by a year. His family always believed that I had been the cause of his breakdown and that I had sacrificed him to my own social advantage in cultivating the Stonors. They, of course, never blamed the pressures they had put on him, however unconsciously, to remain a charming boy, protected from the menacing world of adulthood. Dorothy's rejection had left him feeling less a boy than a failed man.

But at the time, left by myself in the Stonor camp, I gave little thought to the emotional consequences to my friend of the amorous course I had induced him to pursue. I was concentrating my attentions on Guy Thorp.

He was certainly a handsome man. Even I had to admit that. His nose was large and strong and aquiline, and his wavy

blond hair came down in a triangle over a noble forehead as if
to point proudly to the beauty below. His large blue eyes had
a welcoming twinkle, and the robustness of his cheerful laugh
seemed purposed to put an end to any suggestion that he was
too polished, too smooth, to be quite sincere. It did not,
however, put an end to it for me. As I watched the way, at
dinner on the night he arrived, he deferred to his host and
then, just at the point when the table might begin to infer
that he was a toady, the way he would suddenly and effectively
rebut Mr. Stonor's thesis (albeit courteously noting the latter's
"well-known openness to all sides of any question"), I was put
in mind of Decius Brutus's comment on Caesar: "But when I
tell him he hates flatterers, he says he does, being then most
flattered."

The discussion fell naturally on the subject of England,
where Thorp was stationed, and this led to a debate on the
continued expansion of the British Empire. Thorp stoutly de-
fended it, maintaining that Britain with her dominions and
colonies constituted the greatest force for peace in the world.

"I suppose then," Mr. Stonor observed dryly, "that if the
British should extend their empire over the entire globe, our
peace would be assured forever."

"I was only speaking for myself, sir. Actually, I think the
British are more than satisfied with what they already rule. I
get the distinct impression from my friends in Whitehall that
the addition of even one more colony, the very smallest isle or
isthmus, would be regarded as too much of a good thing.
Their whole magnificent administrative system is overworked
as it is."

"That may well be so," his host replied. "But I'm afraid the
growth or shrinkage of empires is a difficult thing to control.
The moment they cease to expand, they start to decline. It's
strange, but there doesn't seem to be any alternative."

I decided it was now my time, if ever, to barge in. What had I to lose? "If the British would like to start shrinking, there's one little emerald isle they might do well to cast off."

The table looked at me in some surprise. My tone, I suppose, had been sufficiently antagonistic.

"Unhappily, it's too close to their shore," Guy responded coolly. "An independent Ireland, able to offer naval bases to Kaiser Wilhelm, would be an unacceptable risk."

His tone was civil enough, but it had a note of experience admonishing naïveté that aroused my ire.

"Ireland could agree not to cede bases. And Britain could easily occupy her if she did. The point is that Whitehall, as you call it, never gives anyone a chance. Look how India was squeezed for the last drop of profit the Raj could get out of her!"

"Surely you go too far there, Leonard. Most trained observers concede that the Raj, as you call it, has spared India a religious war. And I'm sure I don't need to tell anyone here that those wars are the bloodiest."

"Maybe the Indians would rather massacre one another than kiss the British boot!"

"You speak for the killers, I assume. Hardly for the victims." Guy glanced smilingly down the table for the approval he took for granted.

"Whom do *you* speak for, Thorp?"

"How do you mean?"

"Well, to me you sound more like the spokesman for His Imperial British Majesty than for President Taft."

Thorp reddened. "I happen to be a member of the legation that represents the government of the United States at the Court of Saint James's. Does it offend you that I should try to understand and appreciate the great nation to which I have been sent?"

"Not at all. But didn't Bismarck say it was undesirable for his ambassadors to become too fond of the nations to which they were accredited? That's a mistake your friends the British never make."

In the shocked silence that followed this Guy again beamed down the table. "I do believe I've just been insulted!" he exclaimed cheerfully.

Mr. Stonor, who had been watching our little debate with the malice of a man who can enjoy even a protégé's discomfort, now decided I had gone far enough.

"I think we'll have coffee outside," he announced to the hovering butler, for he took even a butler to the wilderness. Dorothy, her face pale with anger, hissed at me to remain when the others went out, and we faced each other under the biggest of the mooseheads.

"Why are you so offensive to Guy? What has he ever done to you?"

"I was trying to show you what a prig he is. You don't know the man."

She gasped. "Look who's talking! Did you ever lay eyes on him before today?"

"Maybe I'm just perspicacious. Maybe I can simply see that you have too much life force to be matched with a man like that. Oh, I don't mean to be too hard on him. I have no doubt he's as brilliant as everyone says. And I'm sure he'd make a perfectly adequate husband for some little woman who'd be content to clap her hands and admire him all her life. But *you!* You don't want to stand at the top of a marble stairway covered with diamonds and be called Mrs. Ambassadress, do you? Your business is living, not strutting."

She stared at me now with something like awe. In the centre of each dark eye was a tiny yellow beam of fascination. I almost laughed aloud. Horace was right! She *was* beautiful. Or might have been, with the right kind of love. Or maybe just with love.

"And on what, pray, do you base this fantastic evaluation of me?"

"On two or three meetings, why not? I have eyes and ears. Enough, anyway, to know that Thorp isn't the man for you."

"And do you have one in mind?"

It was really only then that it struck me, idiot that I was, that Maury Leonard himself might be a candidate for the heiress's hand. Why not? What did her free soul (free, that is, except for the ball and chain that tied her so firmly to the paternal yard) care for money or lineage? No, no, she was honest through and through. But was I? Or was I enough of a sneak to see myself in the role of John Alden?

"Horry, of course."

"Oh, Horry." She turned abruptly away. "Horry and I have reached an understanding about that. And if you can't be civil to Guy, I think you'd better leave."

"I'll do my best!" I called after her retreating back.

My tone had been joking, but my mind was seething with excitement. If I could aspire to such a woman as Dorothy Stonor, I *would* be in love with her! The heroes of legend who rescued princesses from dragons didn't have to have known them for more than a minute to be in love. The nobility of the deed and the rank of the rescued victim were quite enough in themselves to guarantee a true romance. Chivalry was dead only if one thought so. A transit magnate could be a perfectly adequate dragon, and a Yale senior, even a Jewish one, a "parfit gentil knight." Or was I simply disguising my disloyalty to Horace? Had the unreality of Mr. Stonor's palace-cabin in the wilderness converted Dorothy's house party into a masquerade in which all moral rules were suspended?

The following morning, Mr. Stonor, very much to my sur-

prise, invited me to go fishing again. This time he allowed
the guide, who was deaf, to do all the casting and pulling in
while he simply gazed at the scenery. He had a pair of binoc-
ulars and said he was looking for a moose. But this did not
long detain him from the serious topic he obviously wished to
discuss.

"You have made it very clear, Leonard, that you don't
approve of my choice of a son-in-law. I don't of course admit
that it's any of your business, but I'm still interested in your
reasons."

"My only question is whether he's your daughter's choice."

Having invited my confidence, he was in no position to
resent it, nor did he in the least appear to. "She's perfectly
free to reject Thorp if she doesn't fancy him. I can influence
my Dorothy, but I should never try to force her. What have
you against Thorp?"

I hesitated. "You don't think yourself, sir, that he's a bit of
an ass?"

Mr. Stonor was imperturbable. "Because he finds the British Empire a force for world peace? But so it is, for the moment. Thorp is perfectly capable of visualizing that empire in
tatters. You're taken in by his polished manners. He *knows*
how quickly things can change. He has a first-class mind and
the temperament to take him anywhere he wants to go. It
might interest you to know that he worked for me for ten
years before going into the Foreign Service. He could run my
business today."

"Is that what you want him for?"

"Not entirely, no. But I need him to know how. I was the
one who pushed him into the State Department. I want a son-
in-law who'll make a name for himself in public affairs and at
the same time be able to keep an eye on the business. If he

marries Dorothy, I'll see to it that she inherits the controlling shares."

"How will your sons feel about that?"

He didn't bother to express his indifference to this except by a shrug that implied that his male heirs had no one to blame but themselves. "Most rich men are scared their daughters will be married for their money. But it's the man who counts in a son-in-law, not the motive. Naturally a man as ambitious as Guy Thorp is not indifferent to the advantages of becoming my son-in-law. He shouldn't be. I want Dorothy to marry a great man, and I think he has at least a chance of becoming that."

"What about her happiness?"

"I think I can count on Guy for that. He knows that Dorothy is tense and high-strung and that she'll need a lot of affection from her husband and absolute fidelity. It will always be to his interest to give her these, both for the comfort of his own household and for the use of her fortune, over which I shall leave her in complete control. Naturally it's a gamble. What isn't? But I have studied Guy with the greatest care and I believe him to be the sort of man who waxes generous with success. There are such."

"And with failure?"

"He can always be shed. Marriage is no longer a life sentence."

I could not but be impressed at how closely he had worked it all out. I doubted, however, that Dorothy would ever shed a failure, however morose he became.

"You say you're willing to gamble, sir. But with Horace Aspinwall there'd be no gamble. He'd always love her and always be true."

"I'm willing to admit that. I like Horace. He's a fine and

amiable young man. But he will never achieve a first position. He will pick a specialty and be good at it. In the law, for example, he will become a respected partner of his firm, in charge of a minor department. He will never be the senior partner, never a judge or leader of the bar."

"How can you be so sure of that?"

"Aren't you?"

I decided that his candor deserved mine. "Yes. But that can be a good life. Does Dorothy need so much more?"

"Well, you see, I think she does."

"Mightn't she one day, in the grandeur you plan for her, regret Horace Aspinwall and his simpler devotion?"

"Are you really such a sentimentalist, Leonard? You surprise me. Yes, I think she may have occasional regrets. We all do when we waste time thinking about our past choices. But it would be better to regret the simple life, married to Guy, than the glittering one, married to Horace."

Really, the man was a fiend! "I see I'd better give this up," I conceded, reaching for my rod.

"One minute, Leonard. I'm not through with you yet." His voice was sterner now. "I suspect you of flattering yourself that you have made your own impression on my daughter."

"Doesn't every man make his own impression?"

"Don't fence with me, young man. You know just what I mean. And to some extent your self-flattery is justified. Dorothy likes you. Or at least she did until you took that cheap shot at Guy. But even that, in its way, impressed her, or she wouldn't have got so angry."

"You surely don't think I would betray my friend?"

"Would it be a betrayal if his cause was already lost?"

"Anyway, what chance would the likes of me have with a girl like Dorothy?"

"You might have a chance if you could win *my* approval.

But you can't. It's not that I don't suspect that you're going to make your way in this life. And a good way, too. But I don't want a Jewish husband for Dorothy. That has nothing to do with prejudice, of which I am devoid. But socially, being a Jew is still a handicap, and I'm not looking for handicaps in the life I plan for Dorothy. You don't stand a chance with me against you, and I think you know that. But I like you, and if you will go away today and stay away from Dorothy, I'll give a boost to your career when the right time comes."

I stared. I was almost surprised when I heard my own question. "How?"

"Do well in law school, and I'll get you a job with my lawyers."

"In an all-Gentile firm?"

"No, no, they have half a dozen Jewish partners. They have an international practice. That's why it's just the right place for you. An all-Jewish firm wouldn't be broad enough, and an all-Gentile one might never make you a partner. Now of course you're thinking: What if this old geezer dies while I'm still in law school? But I shall exact a moral commitment from my lawyers now. Don't worry. I know I can count on them."

How could a man so intelligent really want his daughter to marry Guy Thorp? But who knew? Maybe he was right there too. I picked up my rod and cast.

"What time does that little train leave, sir?"

2

My story, like *The Winter's Tale,* seems to span two generations, though it is not one of crabbed jealousy redeemed in the lush springtime of a new youth. But if jealousy is not in it,

envy is, or at least the resentment that is cousin-german to
envy. The very considerable worldly success that I enjoyed in
the quarter century that followed my signing up with Hadley
& Jerome (now Hadley, Jerome & Leonard) was only grudg-
ingly recognized by Dorothy, by Gurdon, by (I'm sorry to say)
the older partners of the firm and even by the usually generous-
minded Horace. I have certainly never been a popular man. It
is just as well that I have never trusted anyone but myself to
forge my own way. I would have been a total failure in the
ballot box.

The years from 1911 to 1938 can be summarized. They
represented my growth. What I am basically trying to understand is what seeds were planted in my college days and what
they finally matured into three decades later. Like Chateau-
briand in his memoirs beyond the tomb, I choose to speed up
certain eras of my life and devote whole chapters to others.
Sublime egotist though he was, he recognized that Napoleon
was the principal actor in his own life story. Is it because I am
a greater egotist that I allow no one to dislodge myself from
that position, or only because there has been no Napoleon in
my century?

Horace and Gurdon both became clerks in Gurdon's father's
small but distinguished law firm on Wall Street. On the
death, shortly afterwards, in a single year of three of the senior
partners, the firm was reorganized under the leadership of a
great lawyer-statesman, enlisted largely through Gurdon's
shrewd politicizing, and became the nationally known institution it still is today. There was a fine place for Gurdon in
the new partnership and a secure but far less brilliant one for
Horace, who was encouraged to develop his own little specialty in a restricted field of corporate bonds where the reasonable hours and lack of tension seemed to accord with the needs
of his nervous temperament.

I made every effort to overcome Horace's continuing resentment of me, but had it not been for Gurdon's ugly explosion of temper when his cousin told him he was considering taking a fishing trip with me and his calling Horace the "Jew boy's valet," I doubt I should have succeeded. As it was, Horace and I had a good laugh when he related the details of this little spat, and our old friendship was renewed. And I think we would have enjoyed it to this day had not Dorothy come between us again.

Everything went my way in Hadley & Jerome. I was an associate for only six years before becoming a junior partner. At thirty-five I was a "name" partner and at forty the managing one. As an expert in corporate finance I made a fortune for myself on the market, quite aside from my large fees, and when Mr. Stonor died I was the executor and trustee under his will and director of his charitable foundation. It was widely observed on the Street that Maurice Leonard had a sufficient stranglehold on the Stonor estate without marrying Dorothy. But then I loved Dorothy. I knew people said that I loved where I wanted, but that is love too.

Her marriage to Guy had lasted only three years. She had hoped to keep it patched up at least until her father, aged and ailing, should have died, but Guy had proved too much of a cad for that, and poor Mr. Stonor had the bitterness of surviving to see his best-laid plans in shreds. The only amelioration for him was the possibility that, in mitigation of his own former bad judgment, he might be able to propose his trusted and able favorite as a candidate for successor. Needless to say, I saw what Dorothy's reaction would be to a second paternal champion, and I managed to contain the old man's enthusiasm to suggesting me to his daughter as her divorce lawyer.

She was not at first keen about having an attorney who could say "I told you so," but as she had never gone to any firm but Hadley & Jerome, and as I was the only partner who knew all about her financial matters, she agreed at least to talk to me. And when she found me polite and reserved, yet at the same time tactfully sympathetic, she agreed to the retainer.

It did not take me long to gain her confidence. Like many persons not accustomed to confidences, once the gates were opened for what she deemed a legitimate purpose, then everything tumbled out, almost to her relief. Her marriage had been a sad example of the old American conflict between greed and idealism. How much happier our tycoons and their offspring would have been under the European system of arranged marriages and deaf to the eternal chant of love, love, love! Now, in saying this I of course recognize that an arranged marriage was precisely what Mr. Stonor had sought for Dorothy, but he had reckoned without two considerations which wouldn't have existed for a father in the Old World: one, his daughter's stubborn insistence that hers was a love match, and two, Guy's admittedly unanticipatable adherence to the tough Yankee notion that any "real" man should make his own money. Instead of following his natural bent of cool reason and concentrating on the great career in public life for which Dorothy, inspired by her father, had essentially married him, Guy had quixotically joined a new firm of adventurous investment bankers to engage in a series of disastrous speculations with money borrowed and even (I know, for I later covered it up) embezzled from his wife. His anger over his failures he turned against poor Dorothy, who at last found the courage to close her purse, and the prowess that had done so little for him on the market he turned to other boudoirs, giving her little alternative but to take my advice and divorce him in New York for adultery.

Dorothy's disillusionment had been a shattering experience.

It was almost inevitable under the circumstances that she should have come to regard me, steadfast, trusted, favored by her father, and now her champion against the betrayer, as everything she should have been looking for in the first place in a husband. Did she also harbor the flattering suspicion that I might have remained a bachelor all those years because of unrequited love? We never discussed this, anyway, either then or afterwards, any more than we did my own suspicion that my Jewishness had become romantic to her, exemplifying as it did to her naturally unprejudiced mind ideals much finer than those of the arid and snobbish society to whose standards she had weakly (as she now saw it) submitted. To what more competent hands, to what more proven trustworthy person could she confide her disillusioned self, her little boy and the fortune she had never wanted?

I moved so slowly and cautiously in the matter that no one noticed what was going on but the ever-watchful Horace. He was married himself now, to a plain, tart, nimble-minded little wren of a woman who was totally and protectively devoted to him and indignantly suspicious of anyone who failed in her eyes to give her husband the full due that he was too modest to expect. I think she dreaded the idea of Dorothy's coming back into his life, even as the wife of a friend, and I suspect it was she who egged him on to face me in my office one morning with the grave question: "Are you in love with her, Maury? If you can assure me of that, I have nothing more to say."

I told him that I was, in a tone that he could hardly challenge. And it was true, because I wanted it to be true, and things I have wanted to come true, where I was importantly concerned, for the most part have. I liked and admired Dorothy; I appreciated her character and ideals; I found her person desirable and her conversation amusing. What more was needed for a happy marriage? There was no reason to apprehend the advent of a stronger attachment, for I had never felt a stronger one, and I knew myself pretty well. Nor did Dorothy have any reason to fear losing me for any change in her own circumstances; my loyalty would have been proof against any failure of health or fortune. What more could a woman ask than the confidence that the husband she had chosen could be shed only at her own volition?

Edgar, her little son, was an effete, spoiled brat, but precocious and curiously realistic for his tender age. I think he may have expected me to cultivate his affection, in some clumsy, bearish, vulnerable, stepfatherish way, but I was too shrewd to give him the least opportunity to put me down. I treated him fairly and formally, and through the years he and I have learned to be satisfied with a mild mutual dislike and a mild mutual respect. When Dorothy and I had our own son, Edgar's fondness for his little half-brother opened the possibility of a warmer relationship between us, but Edgar, having (I suspect) considered this, at last rejected it. He always distrusted change.

Dorothy's problem with me had basically the same origin as her problem with Thorp: she could never quite bring herself to accept the fact that her husband was not the man she had imagined. I had fired her imagination as a person independent of a society she had come to despise, and she was reluctant to recognize that my independence was in no way incompatible with a life in the midst of that society. She always confused diplomacy with hypocrisy. She would like to have been marooned with me on a desert island, where I, like the accomplished butler of Barrie's *Admirable Crichton,* though her social inferior in civilized Philistia, would prove a monarch in the wilderness. She found it ignoble that I should manipulate the mean old world of the Stonors and Aspinwalls for our own greater comfort and glory. She could not reasonably object to a handsome style of living compatible with our joint means: the duplex Park Avenue penthouse hung with post-Impressionists and my favorite Fauves, the red brick manor and stables in Virginia, the trim sailing yacht and the fast, rattling foreign cars, but she minded my so loving these things. She was certainly never a political radical, but like some other guilt-ridden heirs of her generation, she tended to believe that the accoutrements of wealth should be accepted as duties rather than pleasures.

As to the wealth itself, her attitude underwent the curious changes I have often, as a lawyer, observed in those who have not had to earn it. At first they make usually futile efforts to dissociate themselves from it: nothing will do but that they must be valued and loved for themselves, whatever *that* may be. But in time they start to adapt themselves to their insidiously comfortable burden and perhaps, in some inner recess of the mind, begin dimly to see it as somehow associated with their own worth, as even, constructively, "earned." To the more serious-minded it becomes an instrument with which to do good, and private luxuries are now balanced with donations to worthy causes. The final step is to convert the wealth into a tool to promote the very ambition it is supposed to have stifled: its possessor becomes a philanthropist who gives his capital only where he can direct the use of the income and where his name will endure on lintels and tablets.

Dorothy reached the last stage after we had been married only a decade. She set up a foundation (under my legal guidance, of course), rented an office, hired a couple of secretaries and proceeded to make large grants to applicants whose appeals she now spent her mornings reading. She disregarded my warning about charitable institutions: that their officers quite sincerely believe that the ends justify almost any means, certainly flagrant misrepresentation, and she was badly taken in by some of her biggest "investments." She would never have discovered this had I not taken care to make the proper investigations, and although she reluctantly complied with my suggestion that she hire a professional director, I don't think she ever quite forgave what she no doubt regarded as a "cynicism" on my part morally inferior to the basic generosity of her own nature.

By 1938, the year of Munich, the year of compromise (I was to have my own), Dorothy and I had long settled into what is sometimes called a "civilized marriage," though the civilization was largely provided by me. We went more and more our separate ways, she spending her days at her foundation and I at my office when I was not travelling on business. At home we had our own bedrooms, and when we entertained it was I who planned the meals with our housekeeper and selected the guests. Dorothy appeared at our parties when she wanted to and accompanied me to others when she chose. Our domestic manners on the whole were good, though she was more inclined to be openly critical than I, and, uncommonly in such a marriage, we had frequent and interesting conversations about the state of the nation and world. But in 1938 a new and acerb note was introduced into our relationship which was to threaten its precarious balance.

Oscar, our only child, who might have been an added bond in a happier union, was instead a source of mutual jealousy. We coveted his affection and resented the careful equality of the love he returned to each of us. For he was the gentlest and justest of youths — I tend to wax maudlin in describing his character. With his looks I am less so, for they were, to say the least, singular. He was skinny and agile, with long thin limbs capable of extraordinary dexterity — he could cross his feet behind his neck. His face, pale and skull-like under short, thick, wiry black hair, was made strangely attractive by the glitter of his green-brown eyes. Intense, romantic and deeply intellectual, he might have been expected to be impatient, abrupt, even caustic, whereas, on the contrary, he was sympathetic and compassionate. With me he was always . . . how shall I put it? Protective? But whom did he wish to protect me from?

In the early spring of that year Oscar was halfway through his course at Columbia Law, and was living at home, his suite in our duplex amounting virtually to a separate apartment. We saw him little enough except on weekends, and it was on a Sunday lunch that I gave for a Chicago investment banker, one Graham Barnes, that Dorothy made the remark that was further to complicate our lives.

We were eight at table, including the Horace Aspinwalls, and our genial and good-mannered banker was questioning Horace with a lively curiosity about the ins and outs of Manhattan social life. He showed a particular interest in a discussion club of which Horace was president, the Thursday Evening Association.

"Do you meet in a clubhouse?"

Horace explained: "No, we meet in the homes of members who have large enough houses or apartments. There we have lectures or musicales or sometimes even a dance. The club goes back to the 'nineties, when the younger members of society began to be restive under the Philistinism of their elders. 'Old New York' was inclined to be nervous about the arts. Richard Harding Davis was acceptable as a writer, and Charles Dana

Gibson as an artist, and to some extent Walter Damrosch could represent music, but that was about the limit. So the Thursday Evening Association was designed to introduce society to the faculty of Columbia! Only, through the years the original purpose and Columbia seem both to have been forgotten."

The banker chuckled. "It sounds not unlike Chicago. You don't find culture at the top of Jacob's ladder. Not yet anyhow. And do you, Maury, attend these affairs?"

"I've been to some, as Horace's guest."

"You're not a member?"

"No."

"How is that, when your pal is president?"

I hesitated. "I guess I figure Horace sees me enough downtown without my intruding on his evening hours."

"I'm afraid, Mr. Barnes, that we're too Jewish for the Thursday Evening Association."

Dorothy's tone was pointed and clear. I think my first reaction was to admire the perfect manners of the table. Nobody betrayed the least surprise. Oscar just glanced in my direction. There was a slight pause before the tactful Barnes put the question to the table as to whether Mrs. Charles Dana Gibson had been the model for the Gibson girl. That his question was immediately answered in unison by all three of the lady guests showed how welcome was the change of subject.

After the guests had departed, I could tell from Dorothy's air of rather defiant apprehension that she was awaiting my reproach, but of course I wasn't going to give her *that* satisfaction. I simply announced cheerfully that Oscar and I had agreed before lunch to walk twice around the reservoir in Central Park that afternoon. He nodded at once, glad to separate his parents, and we set out.

On our first round, on that cold, damp, early spring day, we exchanged hardly a word. Oscar and I had rarely discussed the state of being Jewish. He had never taken the smallest interest in any religion, adhering, like so many intellectual seekers of the truth, to agnosticism if not outright atheism, but he was much concerned with Hebraic history and tradition — he was, in short, a proud Jew. I had been careful, like my own father before me, in confining his education to New York City schools and universities, to minimize his contacts with the cruder forms of anti-Semitism until he should be mature enough to handle them, but I had long since doubted the necessity of this. He seemed from his boyhood to have taken prejudice in his stride, as a curious, objectionable but essentially manageable thing.

On our second round I brought up the topic we had both been waiting for. "Why do you suppose your mother picked today, of all days, to put me down?"

"Put you down, Dad? Couldn't she have been just showing her loyalty to you and me? By identifying herself with our Jewishness?"

"How you try to clean us up, dear boy! But come now, you heard her tone. She was trying to humiliate me. She was telling the table that she at least had nothing to conceal. She might as well have called me a snob and a toady. But why has she waited all these years until now?"

Oscar did me the justice to drop his first line of defense. "I think she's been brooding about it for some time. Waiting for the right moment."

"To stick it to me?"

"Rather to force you into a public stand. She thinks we ought to be more Jewish."

"And you agree?"

"Now, Dad." He stopped, and I stopped. We faced each other, he now the parent. "You know I believe each man must decide these things for himself."

"You don't have the feeling I'm disloyal to my forebears?"

"No!"

"Or a sneaking sense that I've sold out?"

"Look, Dad." He sounded almost exasperated. "You're strong. You don't need anything or anyone in the world but yourself. But other people need all kinds of things: love, patriotism, family, faith, what have you. Mother needs to feel she's socially useful; Uncle Horace that he's good. I guess I need to feel I'm a Jew. It's natural for people to resent your independence. It's envy, really."

I thought this over as we walked on, again in silence. I was interested that he had included Horace among the enviers. Horace had always been very close to his godson, who called him Uncle. Did he consider it a godpaternal duty to counteract what he may have seen as my baleful influence? And then a sickening sense of remorse so overwhelmed me that I suddenly stopped. Had my love of this serious child been simply pride? Had I not essentially left him alone to solve the problems created by my own egotism and splendid — or sordid — isolation? And had he not solved them with the love denied him by both his preoccupied parents?

He had turned and was looking back at me. "You're not going to hold this against Ma, are you?"

"I'm not a grudge bearer. You know that."

"She's not a happy person, I'm afraid. And it's hard for unhappy people not to want to see those around them unhappy, too. Even subconsciously."

"Why do you suppose she's so unhappy?"

"Because everything she's ever cared about — or thinks

she's cared about — has turned out to be unworthy of her ideals."

"Even her sacred father?"

"Oh, him especially."

I nodded. Oscar was certainly shrewd. "But of course we both know who the archvillain is. Do you think, even if I tried, I could ever be anything else to her?"

He turned the question. "No one could ever attain Mother's ideals. If he did, she'd simply up the stakes. Give it up, Dad. Be yourself."

And then, ignoring the preoccupied faces of the rapidly striding pedestrians, he flung his arms around my shoulders and hugged me. My emotion was so strong as nearly to choke me. Independent? That was to laugh. I was horribly vulnerable to this wonderfully loving young man. In my triumph over Dorothy in the contest for his affection I now ruefully realized that victory was Pyrrhic. She had never really contested me; Oscar was essentially a tool to be used in her lifelong campaign to prove that Dorothy was always the wronged one. I had Oscar in the end, but he was a dagger that could be seized and stuck into the centre of my heart.

It was not long after the Sunday lunch of Dorothy's emancipation from tact on the subject of my ethnic origin that Horace Aspinwall came to my office to bring it up again. It appeared that he too had had a talk with Oscar. That Oscar should have had such a discussion with him at all was enough to make me quiver with resentment before I even heard what the principal question had been.

What I now heard Horace say, as coolly as if he were talking about a party or a trip that my son was planning, was this: "Oscar has a project he wasn't sure about broaching to you.

He has this idea about changing his name back to Ullman. He wanted to know how I thought you'd react."

I rose to walk to the window. I needed time for this one. I had first to digest the disagreeable fact that Oscar's relationship with his godfather was a good deal more intimate than I had suspected. I knew he had spent a weekend recently with the Aspinwalls in Greenwich, and I had even wondered whether he might have been attracted to one of their daughters, though both were as gushing and giggly as Horace's sisters had been at the same age. Still, those sisters had married surprisingly well. But a change of name to Ullman would hardly have been the way for Oscar to ingratiate himself with Horace's bustling little country club wife.

"And what did you tell him?" I demanded.

"I told him I thought you would mind, but that you were too sensible to mind very much. And that the decision in any case had to be his own and no one else's."

"Is that *all* you told him?"

"What do you mean?"

I swung around from the window. "Didn't you tell him you *approved* of the idea?"

"I certainly didn't tell him I disapproved."

"Obviously, you think it's a good move on his part. Why?"

"Because I feel that Oscar should be free to assert his identity as a Jew. I needn't tell you how fine a son you have, Maury. He holds his head too high to be associated with the least taint of misrepresentation."

"Unlike his old man, eh?"

"You've always had your own good reasons for doing the things you've done. I'm not going to start criticizing you at this point in our lives."

"You're not?" I stared into those usually gentle eyes, astonished to sense the sudden dislike in them. "I suggest you already have. If you had to pick a son of Dorothy's to make up to you for having none of your own, why couldn't it have been Edgar? Why couldn't you leave me out of it?"

Horace was too shocked at first to answer this. Of course I was being absurd. I was surprised at the violence of my own temper. Edgar would never have had any truck with the likes of poor Horace. He was a languid, indolent homosexual, a frequenter of the highest society, a collector of Greek and Roman sculptures of nude young men. Now Horace tried to reason with a lunatic.

"There was no idea of 'picking' a son of yours, Maurice. Isn't it permissible for a man to be fond of his godson and to want to help him? There are some things that Oscar has found it hard to discuss with either you or Dorothy. She has such pronounced views, and you aren't the easiest person in the world to discuss delicate matters with."

"Why am I not?"

"Just because you can stand there the way you're standing and ask that question the way you're asking it. But let's get back to the point, for heaven's sake. *Would* you really mind so terribly if Oscar became Oscar Ullman?"

"Yes! Because it would hurt him!"

"You mean in the eyes of the world? Why should it? Everyone knows it's his real name. That's the penalty of your fame, Maurice."

"No, I don't mean in the eyes of the world. I don't give a damn about the eyes of the world. I've gotten everything I need from the world." My heart was beating painfully now. "You talk about his real name. What I chose for him is his real name. If he changes it, he will be repudiating his father. He will have created the ridiculous image of a father and son with different family names. And when he sees what he has done, he will suffer what may be a terrible remorse, for he is a very sensitive soul."

"But suppose you change your name, too?"

"Ah, now we have it! Now you're smoked out, Horace! Let the Jew call himself what he is! That's your revenge at last, isn't it, for my muscling in on your unrequited Browning-esque love for Dorothy and taking her for myself? You could never forgive my trying to shake you out of that masturbating passion of yours and showing you how to win the woman you never really wanted!"

"Maury, Maury, you've gone crazy!" Horace shook his head sadly as he slowly rose to his feet. "Let us put a stop to this terrible conversation. You're going to be sorry enough for what you've already said."

"Of course, I don't mean it was all conscious on your part," I said lamely.

"At least we have decided one thing." He turned back from the door. "There can be no further question of Oscar's changing his name. Certainly not in *your* lifetime."

So he had the last word, after all. I guess I have always underrated Horace.

The outbreak of war in Europe effected a curious change in my former best friend. Horace became the most concerned and vocal of interventionists. I wondered whether Armageddon didn't seem to offer him a possible escape from the long little-ness of his life. I suppose this was true of many men. We had both been in Officers Candidate School in 1918 when the war had ended, depriving us of our chance for combat in France, as much to my relief as to Horace's chagrin. I had been eager only to get on with my career. But now, in 1940, Horace was always plaguing me with his plans to take a leave of absence and go to England in any assisting capacity. As the United Kingdom had no urgent need of American males in their fifties, except to promote war feeling and military aid in their own country, he spent his days in interventionist committee meetings, organizing huge rallies in halls draped with the banners of the occupied nations. Dorothy joined him with the exaltation born of finding a cause worthy of all her shattered ideals. So they were together at last in a union that even Horace's disgruntled little wife could not openly object to. They could both exclaim, like the dying Henry James, "At last, the distinguished thing!"

The war had an equally strong but less heady effect on Oscar. He was a lawyer now and still living at home, but not working, for he had planned a year's trip around the world which Hitler's invasion of Poland had interrupted. He became almost sombre and much less communicative. He spent his days largely in his own rooms, reading or listening to records of his beloved Bach, and his nights in bars with unmarried friends who worked in the day. As he didn't drink, his need for discussion with his contemporaries had to be compelling.

The crisis that was clearly pending broke one morning when he appeared in my office, solemn of mien.

"I'm going to Canada, Dad. I want to enlist in the RAF or the RCAF, whichever will take me."

The razor that had been encased in my heart ever since Oscar had started taking flying lessons now turned over.

"Can't you wait until we get in?"

"But *will* we?"

"If your mother and godfather have anything to do with it, we will." I had seen them as pathetic, even a bit ridiculous; now I saw them as menacing.

"Ma and Uncle Horace have an awful lot of isolationists to

fight. And maybe the isolationists have a point. Maybe it's not their war. All I know is it's mine."

"You mean it's a Jew's war."

"I'm not trying to convert anyone. It's a war for *me* as a Jew. The little man with the moustache is doing his best to exterminate us."

"Does your mother know your plan?"

"Yes, and she's being very Roman about it. Uncle Horace tells me I'm doing what he'd do if he were my age. He says he envies me."

"I wish to hell he *was* your age!" I almost shouted. "What the hell are they trying to do? Ship you off to your death before I can stop you?"

"Now, Dad, calm down. They're both very much concerned as to how you'll take it."

"And well they might be!" We argued, I heatedly and he coolly, for the rest of the morning and through lunch. The only thing I was able to obtain was a delay until September. It was now June, and France had fallen. My clinching argument was that if we were suddenly dragged into the war, our air force would desperately need pilots. I did *not* tell him that I feared Britain would now go under and that my requested delay in his plans might spare his going under with her.

"And what shall I do in the meantime?" he asked sullenly.

"Come and work in the firm for the summer. I'll see you get something interesting to do."

But he didn't want to work for me; he preferred, he said, to be on his own. Was it because he begrudged me his concession? Our most important decisions are based on trivia. He consulted Horace, and Horace suggested he apply to his firm. Had I known of this, I would have raised heaven and earth to stop him. I learned of it, however, only when Oscar again presented himself in my office, this time flashy-eyed and tight-lipped. He had been refused a job by the hiring partner of Gurdon and Horace's firm.

"I suppose they give summer jobs only to second-year law students," I suggested in a voice that concealed my desperation.

"That was what Mr. Otis said. But that was not the real reason." Of course it wasn't. Oscar had stood in the first ten of his class in law school and had been an editor of the review.

"Why should you doubt him?"

"Because on my way out I dropped in to see a classmate who's been working there a year. He's a pal and put it to me straight. Otis had shown him my application and asked him about me. He said he was thinking of recommending to the firm that they make an exception in their no-Jews policy. My friend and I could only assume that Otis had been overruled by the hiring committee."

"Have you told this to Horace?"

"Yes. Just now. He was frightfully upset. He said he'd talked to his cousin Gurdon, and that Gurdon had assured him it would be all right. Uncle Horace thought I would be proud to be the first to make them lift the bar. But I guess Gurdon, like Otis, couldn't swing it."

"Assuming he even tried! Assuming this wasn't his way of humiliating me, getting back at me for old scores! Goddamm Gurdon Aspinwall! And goddamn your godfather, too!"

"Dad, I'm sure Uncle Horace, at least, meant well. But do you see what this means? One of the most distinguished firms in the country turns down a qualified candidate — and the son, too, of a man who could help them, or even hurt them — simply to preserve unblotted their perfect record of never taking a Jew! Dad, I'm off to Canada tomorrow!"

*   *   *

And that is how I lost my son. In Canada he was found a capable enough aviator to be sent directly to England, where he was commissioned in the RAF and killed in an air battle over London, his second of time in Britain's finest hour.

For a while I didn't care what happened to me. I went through my days at the office, spending more and more time there, performing my tasks automatically, though enough like my old self for my partners to think I was a stoic, if indeed they did not rather suspect I was simply hardhearted. Dorothy was afflicted, but much less than I; I doubt she had ever really loved anyone since Guy Thorp's betrayal.

Besides, she found exaltation in the role of a dead hero's mother; it dramatized and elevated her sale of war bonds. But I will admit that she seemed to sense my agony with an uncharacteristic compassion. She may have felt, not that she had helped to drive Oscar to his death, but that I might believe she had. Oddly enough, she may have preferred a hating Maurice to an indifferent one. But then she was always an exception to her own rules.

Horace had begged my forgiveness, almost on his knees, for the fiasco with his firm. I could only offer my pardon formally, to be rid of his lugubrious presence.

"Don't flatter yourself that you had anything to do with Oscar's enlistment," I couldn't help adding. "It was entirely a matter between him and Hitler."

Some weeks later, when I encountered Gurdon in the washroom of a downtown lunch club, a hotter scene occurred. I had meant not to speak to him at all, but he sidled up to my wash stand with a long countenance.

"Maury, I can't tell you how sorry I was about your son. We thought he was the finest fellow in the world. Of course, we don't give summer jobs to fully fledged lawyers, but we were planning to offer him a full-time one as soon as the war was over."

And there, in the presence of all those middle-aged and elderly hand-washing and urinating gentlemen, I spat in his mournful face. It was one of the more satisfactory moments of my life.

It seemed for a long while that all the things I had achieved in life were simply the vanities of which the sages speak. I almost wanted it to be so. What was the point of living in a world where the Oscars were killed and the Gurdons survived? I tried to take a gloomy pleasure in my own futility. But my egotism, like the cheerfulness of Doctor Johnson's friend, was always breaking in. I could not blind myself to the fact that some Oscars would survive a war fatal to many Gurdons. And the day came when, standing before my great Gauguin of a yellow idol on a green beach by a red sea, I congratulated its astute purchaser. The following week, in Virginia, I visited my stables and recognized my revived affection for my beautiful horses. There was talk now of my receiving an important post on the War Production Board. I was coming back to life in spite of myself. Or was it, really, in spite of myself?

HEPHAESTUS

God of Newfangled Things

TUXEDO PARK, some forty miles northwest of New York City by beautiful Sterling Forest, was still, in the autumn of 1948, a reservation of large estates where some of the richer burghers of Manhattan could escape the urban heat or crush in summer or on weekends, protected, like the ancient Chinese, from the invasion of intruders by a long encircling wall and a guarded gate. In this House of Mammon were many mansions, and of many styles, most of them now weatherbeaten and maintained less lavishly than in the *belle époque,* but still making a brave enough show to impress the houseguest, and it was generally conceded that old Humphrey Kane's little gem of a French Renaissance château, designed in the 'twenties by his nephew Gilbert, before the latter went "modern," was the prize of them all.

Humphrey's wife, Heloise, a generation younger than her husband and half-French to boot, had worked closely with his nephew in planning the house, inspired by Azay-le-Rideau on the Loire, and in laying out the grounds, which included a

moat, a formal garden and a maze. There were those who had
not scrupled to say that the whole undeniably beautiful place
was a monument to their illicit passion. But that was more
than two decades ago. Gilbert Kane in 1948 was sixty, with a
fashionable wife and four teenage children, and his uncle, a
hale ninety, no longer seemed unseasonably old for his now
fading spouse. When the Gilbert Kanes arrived to spend an
October weekend with their relatives to discuss the proposed
demolition of the now obsolete servants' wing and the reorgan-
ization of the *corps de logis* to make it manageable by a hired
couple, only the oldest residents of the Park wondered whether
Olive Kane still harbored any jealousy of her aunt-in-law, or
whether old Humphrey yet kept a wary eye on his nephew.

Certainly Gilbert, circling the house alone in the chilly
twilight of that Saturday, was not thinking of his uncle's wife.
He was utterly absorbed in the contemplation of his early
work, and his heart ached as he took in, with each new vista,
a further and deepening reassurance of its continuing lightness
and loveliness. American houses of the Beaux Arts school, even
the best of them, even those of Hunt and White, had always
struck him as tending with time to take on a dank, heavy,
institutional quality, which had been a principal reason for his
giving them up in favor of contemporary styles. But now it
actually began to seem to him that he may have constituted a
blessed exception to that rule, that it may have been his
unique distinction to transport the spirit of the European
country manor to the West in such a way as to enhance and
even enrich what Henry James had called the "thin American
air."

But few, alas, of his earlier creations had not been destroyed
or perverted. His proud Roman villa in Bernardsville, New
Jersey, was now a scrubby college sprouting two grotesque
dormitory wings. His serene Irish manor house in Westbury,

Long Island, like a sleek racehorse harnessed to a hay wagon, served as the "social centre" of the housing development clustered thickly around it. And the romantic, rambling Jacobean mansion that had commanded a rocky peninsula on Mount Desert Island was a heap of ashes after the great Bar Harbor fire of the preceding year.

Still, his masterpiece remained before his vision, or would until he had fulfilled his uncle's commission. Its chaste white front under the high gabled windows and turrets of its roof seemed to cast a reproach at him over the glinting moat and the pale park in the darkling air. Never had he conceived a more perfect thing! There was no way he could remove a shutter or add a window without marring the harmony of the whole. Returning now to the house, he knew he would have to tell his uncle to get another to do his dirty work.

He entered the parlor by a French window and found the other three seated by the fire, as if they had been waiting for him. His uncle, rigid, gaunt and brown, with snowy hair, rarely spoke these days, though his mind, once largely occupied in multiplying a modest inheritance, like a shiny tool kept in a velvet case, was still in perfect order. Heloise, interrupted by his entrance in something she was saying to Olive, let her arms, which she no doubt had been using in an emphatic Gallic gesture, drop to her sides. She was painfully thin and too pale, and her hair was almost absurdly gold. Olive, nearly as trim and straight as when she had married Gilbert, her lineless face bearing only a hint of marble, had no need to be concerned. But her small piercing eyes told the advent of the mood of apprehension with which she so constantly had to grapple.

"This house is the best thing I've ever done!" he exclaimed too loudly. "It's a shame to slice off even one room."

His uncle shrugged. Heloise murmured something about

eight servants' rooms being a lot for a couple. Olive came straight to the point, *her* point, anyway.

"What does it tell you about our marriage," she demanded in the cool, mocking tone that had helped to make her reputation as a wit, "that Gilbert thinks his best work was done in his bachelor days?"

"It tells me that he was dreaming about the lovely girl he would one day marry," Heloise suggested, in a tone too bright.

Gilbert sighed. Why could Olive never endure the idea that he might have had even a moment of true satisfaction before the advent of her love? It was his cue to inundate her with affectionate reassurance, but the vision of the façade and moat was still too strong in his mind, and he breached, even brutally, his old habit.

"It's perfectly true! I *did* do better work then. Much better than anything I've done since." But the instant agony in her eyes smote him. "I don't suppose it was just being a bachelor," he added lamely. "It may have been youth."

Heloise took it all in, perhaps a touch maliciously, glancing from husband to wife. Then she turned to her own.

"Come, Humphrey, dear, it's time for your nap. He always takes one before dinner," she explained as she led the old man to the hall.

Alone with her husband, Olive wasted no time. "It's better out in the open." Her tone was sharp and clipped. "Let's face it. You *were* happier back then. Much happier. What did you need an expensive wife for, or four expensive children? What did you care for being the maker of Clinton Village or Knickerbocker City? All you wanted was to build fancy villas for your rich friends and hear them praised by your silly old aunt! Busybody that I was! I should have left you alone."

"Olive, Olive . . ."

"And I wish to God I had!" Her voice rose to a wail as she shut her eyes and clenched her fists.

"Olive, darling, you know that's all perfect nonsense. Those villas were doomed anyway. Are you forgetting the Depression? I'd have had to go into public building whether or not we'd married. Uncle Humphrey was the only Kane who wasn't bust."

"No, no, bachelors can always get by. You'd have had all those free meals and weekends. Maybe there wouldn't have been as many private houses being built, but there'd have been some, enough for you anyway. And you'd have been happy, perfectly happy!" She patted her nose and eyes with her handkerchief. It was the sign that remorse was following anger. "I should never have interfered with your life."

"Olive, you're being ridiculous. You know how I love you and the children. I couldn't do without you."

"Maybe not now. But I'm talking about then. Oh, I know you love us in your own way." She put away her handkerchief; now she would try to be fair. "I shouldn't have been mean about your houses. They *are* works of art. Great art, I'm sure. And you're probably right. They may well be what you should have been doing all these years. Very well then, let's go back to them." Oh, she would make up to him now if it killed her! "You don't have to spend all your time on housing developments and shopping centres. There must be a hundred ways we could cut down on our style of living without even feeling it."

Maybe it was only a game, but it was one that he was very much tempted to play. "But nobody wants the kind of houses I used to build. 'Derivative' has become a dirty word."

"Among our friends, perhaps. They have to be modern. But

the new rich aren't all that way. Read your house and garden
magazines. In Dallas and Houston, they tell me, there are
areas where you might be floating down the Loire."

Gilbert was struck by the truth of what she was saying. In
his office, only the week before, he had been trying to persuade
a client planning a new house in Greenwich that he would do
better to follow Frank Lloyd Wright than Palladio. But suppose he should show the client on Monday his old portfolio of
the villas he had drawn during his stay in Vicenza in 1924?

"You know, darling, you have an idea there. You really
have."

And he was sure that his violent spouse would now expend
as much energy in making him pick up the past as she had in
her youth, when she induced him to drop it.

2

In 1927, at age thirty-nine, Gilbert was still a bachelor. He
had always tolerated the notion, clamped firmly but unobtru-
sively to the back of his mind, that he would marry at forty.
He favored what he liked to think of as the European point of
view, that a man should keep the best years of his life for
himself. His concept of the young American suburban marriage, with a youthful father throwing balls to little boys on
the lawn or taking a noisy rabble of kids with a barking
Airedale for a Sunday drive, had little appeal for him. Of
course he wanted, in due time, to have a lovely younger
woman to be the congenial partner and charming hostess of
his middle and later years and a couple of well-brought-up
children to be the delight and support of his senescence, but
there was no rush about these things, and he was not such a

fool as not to realize that any family that fate should accord him might be very different from his projected ideal. He was, after all, a very social creature, and he had observed, at close enough quarters, several of his friends' marriages falling apart.

Though "pushing forty," he still felt youthful; he had kept his tall muscular figure and all of his wavy auburn hair. He played squash in the winter and tennis in the summer; he drank moderately and never smoked; and his success as the designer of private houses and his popularity as a man about town provided a civilized blend of work and pleasure which it seemed folly even to think of interrupting. Might not a man in such good shape put off the fateful decision until forty-five? Or even fifty?

His friends and relations, however, and particularly the widowed mother whose only child he was, had a very different theory as to the cause of his prolonged unmarried state. They placed the blame, articulately voiced to all ears but those of Humphrey Kane, squarely at the door of the latter's younger wife, at whose smart new house on Sutton Place, overlooking the East River, her nephew-in-law and near contemporary called every evening on leaving work.

She was always alone when he came. There would be a bright fire and tea things on a little table, to be followed, after the consumption of a single cup, by the butler with the cocktail tray. Heloise was not so much beautiful as exquisite. Her blond hair and wide opaque eyes and pale luminous skin might have evoked a sense of serenity had they not been balanced by her darting gestures and the vivid mobility of her facial expressions, which announced the accomplished *maîtresse de maison,* and by the low musical voice that constituted so perfect an instrument for her fine intelligence.

"Do you know, my dear," she asked him on an evening which seemed for her to be a kind of summing up, "that this is my favorite part of the day?"

"Mightn't that be because it's mine?"

"Oh, you don't have to say that. I wasn't fishing. And I suppose it's a mistake to chatter about the things one really loves. They sound smaller when you try to put them into words. But the two of us here by the fire, with the slight lift of the cocktail and with our beloved understanding that it's just this and doesn't have to be anything else at all . . . ah, it's time suspended, it's magic! But how I go on. Tell me to shut up. Tell me about your day. How is the house in Syosset coming? Did you solve the problem of the tower?"

"No. Except that I may eliminate it. It was a quiet day. Nothing at all, really. Oh, except that Mother called. She wants me for dinner on Monday. I said I was going to the opera with you and Uncle Humphrey, but she insisted she absolutely *had* to have me and promised she'd square it with you."

It was their tacit understanding that she would always release him. "That's quite all right. We'll be four without you, so there'll be three in the front row. You know Cousin Polly's rule when she gives you her box. No gaps in the diamond horseshoe! But why is your mama so desperate?"

"It's always the same thing. She's got some sweet little body she wants me to meet."

"She never gives up, does she?"

"Do you imply she should recognize that the case is hopeless?"

"Not at all. I haven't the slightest doubt that you will marry when *and whom* you wish."

"At any rate she will be a young lady who is glad to recognize your place in my life. One who will know how much she has to gain by your friendship."

"Oh, my dear Gilbert, you don't know our sex if you really believe *that*. She will want my head on a silver platter. That's fine. She shall have it. But not yet. No, not quite yet. Never fear. I shall know the time when it comes."

The more delicate-minded among the acquaintance of Heloise and Gilbert preferred to describe their relationship as an *amitié amoureuse;* the more earthy called it an affair. Gilbert took a pleasure which his mother found perverse in the confusion of his observers. He felt it important for himself as an artist to be in constant touch with a fascinating and sympathetic woman, to be able to tell her what he was building and dreaming of building, to discuss with her the current books both were reading, to laugh, not always with malice, at the foibles and pretensions of their nearest and dearest, and to rejoice with her in a world where he was able to do the only work he cared about and have her appreciate it with a pleasure so obviously genuine that he was not obliged to feel selfish. But it was also important for him to feel that he had not neglected the imperious call of romance to the eyes of a world disposed to consider it an essential part of the "real" life of every man and woman.

This was where Heloise was perfect; she never made him feel that he offered her too little or too much. He knew that, like himself, a true artist at heart, she made little distinction between appearance and what the crowd called reality. She was the product of two very different societies, and she had learned at an early age that one can seem anything to others that one wishes to seem. Her father, an American puritan and a lecher, had married, in the Paris of the 'eighties to which he had emigrated in pursuit of pleasure, a pearl of the demimonde

with a passion for respectability. Each had been cruelly disillusioned. She had wanted to move to New York, where her
past might not be known, and he, a stubborn expatriate, had
been disgusted to find that marriage had not made her acceptable to the American colony in Paris. They had already separated when he died of a venereal disease, and his family had
reclaimed little Heloise against a maternal opposition motivated only by cupidity and brought her up in New York. It
was not, however, her shrewd and worldly old paternal grandmother, but Heloise herself, an alert and sharp-eyed young
lady, sophisticated beyond her years, who had decided that
marriage to Humphrey Kane, twice her age, was probably the
best that the child of a bankrupt father and a disreputable
mother could expect. She was wrong. New York memories of
the past, particularly a trans-Atlantic past, were soon faded;
she could have made a younger and equally advantageous
match. But true to her Gallic blood, she carried out her side
of the bargain, and no one ever dared offer a hint about her
and Gilbert to the latter's infatuated old uncle.

Heloise now thought of another point to make in their
discussion of Gilbert's mother's matchmaking.

"Your father was older than Humphrey, you know. He was
older than you are now when he married your mother. Why
must she be so impatient?"

"She thinks I should be making babies. She has rather a
thing about that."

"But she made only one herself!"

"Maybe that's just it. Maybe she wants me to make up for
her deficiency."

"Oh, Gilbert, be serious. You must admit it's a curious
obsession for a woman of the world. And that's what she is,
you know. She cuts a considerable figure in society."

"All hundred and eighty pounds of her."

"I certainly wasn't referring to *that*. And anyway, she carries her weight with a kind of majesty. Those shiny black curls and that stately stride. And that wonderful rich deep voice . . . at times I actually envy her."

"At times."

"I'm serious, Gilbert! And she enjoys all the good things of life. I'm sure, for example, that she takes the greatest pride in your work."

"Well, I think she *does* appreciate it, yes. She has taste, despite her rather florid style of living. But I feel she suspects a devil lurking behind anything *too* beautiful. A devil that may be preventing the artist from performing his proper domestic role."

"Like making babies?"

"Yes! Art to her is like a tame leopard walking gracefully at your side, but muzzled and on a strong leash. If it ever gets loose, it may chew up babies and spouses and cozy cottages and all the warm cuddly things any 'real' life should be full of."

"What a concept!" Heloise raised her hands in dismay. "But wasn't there a time when she herself was concerned with artistic things? Didn't she have stage aspirations as a girl? I seem to recall the story of a recitation before the great Réjane herself."

"It's perfectly true. When my grandparents were living in Paris, because Grandpa was working on his monumental life of Napoleon, Mother, who, believe it or not, was then a slip of a girl, learned to recite French classic drama with great skill and effect. And one evening when Réjane was at the house, my grandmother had the nerve to bring her daughter downstairs to recite a *tirade* from *Phèdre*. Réjane was so struck that she offered to take her under her wing and train her! And poor Mother was dying to do it. But my grandfather, who was a bit of a despot, like his biographical subject, was certainly not going to expose his virgin daughter to the *louche* stage world of Paris. No sirree! The sobbing girl was trundled straight home and married off to poor old Dad."

"But, Gilbert, they loved each other!"

"Did they? Or rather did she? She was certainly good to him, particularly in his long painful last illness. But I've always nursed the fanciful notion that she kept a hot little flame burning inside her, walled up behind that solid flesh. And that when you hear that rich deep voice of hers announcing some spicy bit of society gossip, she may be inwardly declaiming: '*Ah, cruel, tu m'as trop entendu . . . Connais donc Phèdre et toute sa fureur!*' "

"Which should make her then understand the needs of an artist."

"Or how important it is to circumvent them!"

He saw at once that he had been perfectly right about his mother's dinner party. There were eight guests besides himself, seven of whom had been invited in a vain attempt to disguise the fact that he had been asked to meet the eighth. She was Olive Payson, a trim, handsome, dark-haired woman, of presumably undoubted competence in everything she did, who might have been twenty-nine for a couple of years now.

His mother explained her briefly. "She's going to do over this room and the dining room. I'm told she's the cleverest decorator in town. Doesn't insist I have to get rid of everything. 'This house is *you*, Mrs. Kane.' I like that. No fancy pants."

Gilbert certainly agreed that the house *was* his mother. It had been the old Kane family mansion, tall, high-ceilinged, full of huge cabinets and jardinières, with potted palms in corners, more like a French commercial art gallery than a residence, but his mother, with her ample figure and high-piled glistening black hair, her big flat pearls and rich brocaded gown, fitted it like another jardinière.

"She's charming-looking," he conceded.

"And with a mind like —"

"I know. A steel trap," he finished for her. "Like the one you want to catch me in. Don't overdo it, Ma."

"She's too good for you. That's for sure."

"She'd better be. Or I won't look at her."

Like all the girls his mother picked out for him, she was the opposite of Heloise. Why were women supposed to be subtle?

The dinner party was one lady short, so Gilbert had on his other side a deaf old bachelor cousin. That too had been an obvious maternal design. He could talk throughout the meal with Olive.

She told him that she had recently redecorated rooms in two of his houses.

"It's a delight to work in such beautiful buildings, even if they set a tough standard for a decorator to live up to. Which is your favorite, of all your houses? Or don't you have one?"

"I'm like a mother with a large brood. It's always the newest baby."

"Do you confine your practice to private houses?"

"Pretty much so. I did a country club last year, but that was along the same lines, I guess."

"No schools? No office buildings? No factories?"

"You sound as if you might find me trivial."

"No, no. It's not that I have anything against villas. Only don't they represent a rather limited section of our society?"

"Aren't the best things usually limited?"

She nodded, but didn't return his smile. "But even if your houses are the best of their kind — and I have no doubt they are — mustn't they still represent a culture that's past?"

"You mean dead and gone? Well, if Brunelleschi and Palladio and Adam and Mansart are dead and gone, then I am too. And glad to be!"

"I don't mean to take anything away from those old masters. But shouldn't a man of your genius sometimes speak for his own era?"

Decidedly, he was going to like this young woman. "Leaving my 'genius' aside, are you telling me I ought to go 'modern'?"

"Well, not exclusively, of course. But in the age of the skyscraper, I think it would be a sorry thing if Gilbert Kane was not at least represented."

This was the note on which Olive began and which she continued to strike on the evenings when he took her out to dinner, at one expensive restaurant after another.

Never in his life before had an emotional relationship developed in so sure and speedy a fashion. Olive made him feel they had been destined to be close to each other like two characters in the first act of a romantic comedy, the happy ending of which is taken for granted. She took hold of him as easily and firmly as if she had been prepared for the role. Yet that was not possible; she had met his mother only the month before. She was never in the least hurried; when she bade him good night, reaching in her purse for her latchkey, the swift little peck of a kiss she gave him on the cheek seemed more the expression of a pleasant proprietorship than any anticipation of deeper delights. They talked about everything from architecture to the repeal of Prohibition, and about all the people it turned out they knew in common, except two. He never spoke of Heloise, and she never mentioned his mother.

The Humphrey Kanes went to Palm Beach every winter, but this year they had gone early, and Gilbert's mother with them. Had she badgered Heloise into advancing the date on some plea that Humphrey should escape the unusually low temperatures of the season? And could Olive have *known* of that? At last he ventured a reference.

"There's someone I'd love to have you meet when she gets back to town."

"I know. Your aunt. I've heard of her fabulous charm. I'm terrified she'll find me a hayseed."

"You? How ridiculous! She'll delight in you."

"I doubt that." And now, for the first time, she gave him an appraising glance, a look that seemed to be asking just how far, after all, they had come. "I rather fancy she may tell me that she wants her nephew back."

"Has he been away?"

"I hope so."

"Far away?"

"I'm hoping that too."

He smiled, took her hand, which was resting on the table, and held it a moment. "Heloise can have him back only if you come with him."

She didn't return his smile. "Do you mean a package deal?"

"Maybe something like that."

"Oh, no." Her headshake was firm. "I wouldn't share you."

"What a funny girl you are! I have no idea what you feel about me. Am I just the suave older man with whom it's fun to talk about art and such things over a good meal, or am I —"

Her interruption was sharp and definite. "Don't ask me that, Gilbert. Don't ask me anything like that. Wait until you're very sure about your own feelings. I don't talk about mine because if I let them out of the bag, I might not be able to put them back. I warn you: I can be a violent woman. When I care, I care a lot. But I don't throw myself at anyone. No one gets what he hasn't asked for."

He winced. "Couldn't you put it just a wee bit more romantically?"

"No, Gilbert, I play fair."

He was a good deal put off by this and didn't call her for two days. But then in the middle of a snowy afternoon, as he was sitting over his drafting board, the idea suddenly and shockingly presented itself, as if in huge black capital letters — right there between his staring eyes and his drawing of a wing to a bathing pavilion — that if he let this girl go, he might never, never find anyone to match her. For where in the name of matrimony was he going to encounter the combination of so fine a mind and so fine a body with such extraordinary sympathy and so unprecedented an interest in his own silly self? True, she had warned him she could be violent, but what did that mean except that she was capable of jealousy, and why should he ever have to give her cause for that?

He telephoned her at her office. "I want to marry you," he heard himself blurt out.

A long silence ensued. "I'll tell you what, Gil. I'm going to Palm Beach tonight on a big job. The house is vast, and I'll be there at least two weeks. That should give you time to think this over. In the meantime I shan't regard you as in the least committed. We can talk when I get back."

Why was it, he wondered afterwards, that he was suddenly grateful for the delay? Was it anything more than the last desperate reassertion of the doomed bachelor within him, the squeaking prayer for one more chance?

*   *   *

Two days after Olive's departure Heloise telephoned to say that she and his uncle were back. When he called on her that afternoon at his usual time, she startled him with her exclamation.

"I admired her!"

"Do you mean Olive?"

"Of course I mean Olive. She came to see me in Florida, the day before we left. Very good of her, I'm sure, considering how busy she must be with that ghastly pile of Mrs. Slade's. She told me what wonderful friends you and she had become."

"What else did she tell you?"

"Oh, she didn't have to tell me anything else. I'm not blind, you know. But I do think, in view of our poor old friendship, that you might have given me a hint of this *grand amour* of yours. I shouldn't have felt quite such an antiquated slipper."

"I'm sure Olive didn't make you feel that."

"But it's just what she *did* do, in her own wonderful way!" He saw now that Heloise, the always equable, was actually shivering with anger. "It was really quite marvellous how many things she had going for her: youth and purity and promise. I could only clutch a rag around the nudity of my years. But, as I said, I had to admire her. All she had to do was stand there, like the Statue of Liberty — and I fear in time even her lovely figure will take on some of that solidity — holding up the lamp of the future to scan my poor features!"

"I can't believe she said anything rude."

"She didn't. On the contrary, she was most polite. I am to be always welcome in the home of the new Gilbert Kanes."

"She said *that!*"

"Not in so many words, of course not. We women understand each other. What she conveyed very clearly was the message that if I will be so good as to resume my role of venerable aunt, I may expect to be treated with respect and even affection, and be visited on family occasions."

Gilbert was silent as he contemplated the bleakness of the prospect. Why were women supposed to provide the color in life? "And what if I don't choose to go along with what you inferred were Olive's terms?"

"Oh, but you must! She's what is best for you. She's quite right about that. And so is your mother. Everyone is quite right. You and I must bow to the inevitable. To the goddesses of the harvest and fecundity. To all that replenishes this poor old earth!" Her laugh jangled bitterly. "I must be like the man in the Browning poem. I can only plead for one more last ride together."

But with this she rose and came swiftly over to him to stoop down and kiss him, for the first time, passionately on the lips.

The "last ride" was certainly a unique experience. It lasted ten days, during which Heloise came three times to his apartment at noon, which she called "the Manhattan businessman's adultery hour." She drew the curtains in the bedroom, preferring the semidarkness, as she was careful to explain, not because of her age but because she associated romance with twilight. She amazed him with her voluptuousness, with the ease and grace of her performance. Was it a performance, which she had for years been rehearsing in her imagination, so that, stepping suddenly on the stage of reality, she was an accomplished actor? Or was it some inheritance from her mother, locked away in safe storage through the years of a cold marriage and preserved intact for the day it was needed? She even managed to make their lovemaking seem the normal and always anticipated consequence of their long *amitié amoureuse.*

And yet. There was not only the guilt of his betrayal of Olive, in no way assuaged by her refusal to commit herself. There was his uneasy sense of being enmeshed in something a bit sickly sweet, something like a nineteenth-century French academic painting of a Roman banquet, with white robes slipping off the alabaster limbs of languidly reclining ladies. And there were moments in his office, leaning over his drafting board, his mind far from his work, when his cheeks would burn as he imagined in what language his young assistants might be discussing him: "They say the old coot can't find anyone to fuck but his aunt." And then he pictured his mother, as she had been when he was twelve, stalking majestically into his bedroom to catch him in the act of masturbation.

And the house he was working on. The rose-pink, color-washed Baroque villa for the seaside in Boca Grande, a glowing echo of the Portuguese palace of Queluz, the future jewel of his Florida collection. Was it really beginning to strike him as something musty and faded, like a desiccated petal preserved between the leaves of an old quarto?

Olive called him at his office the day before her scheduled return. He was so startled by the sudden sound of her voice that he couldn't imagine where she might be.

"Where are you? In Palm Beach?"

"No, I'm back. I came home a day early. I decided that I wanted you to take me to dinner."

All he could think of was that he wasn't ready to see her. Not at all ready. It was simply too soon, he thought with something like panic, much too soon.

"I'm afraid I'm not free tonight."

"What are you doing?"

His mind was a cipher. "I . . . I have to work."

"Then your mother was right!" Her voice was pebbly. "She telephoned me to come back."

"Come back for what?"

"Come back to see what your old slut of an aunt was up to. I don't believe for a minute you have to work tonight. You're meeting her, aren't you?"

"I am not!" he replied, in all honesty, but with a guilty emphasis.

"Then I'll give you one more chance. Will you take me to dinner tonight?"

"I . . . I . . . well . . ."

She hung up.

He was distraught. There was no question of any more work that day. He went home; he went out again; he roamed the streets. The image of Olive had now become a Diana, bold, beautiful, flashing-eyed, fleet of foot, with tight firm flesh and a bow and arrow, ready to seek a noble prey. Had he lost her forever, this wonderful creature, through his own weakness and folly? In his desperation he called on his mother.

"Why did you tell Olive to come back? Do you realize you may have destroyed my one chance for a happy marriage? What devil in you makes you frustrate your own plans?"

"I knew exactly what I was doing. And I'll try to make things right for you if you'll give me your word never to see Heloise again."

"Never?"

"Except of course as an aunt. And only when your uncle is with her."

He stared in astonishment at those snapping black eyes. How could she possibly have learned what was going on? Did she and Heloise discuss such things? Did he know *what* women talked about?

"I'll have to see her once more. To tell her what I've promised you."

"Just once? Your word of honor?"

"My word of honor."

"Very well. I'll see what I can do with Olive. But it isn't going to be easy." She cast her eyes to the ceiling in mute appeal. "Men can be such asses."

Gilbert found his uncle alone when he called the next day, in the room where he was always received by Heloise, and there was no evidence of tea things.

"Sit down, Gilbert. You will agree that I have been a most tolerant uncle. I have at all times taken into consideration how much younger Heloise is than myself, and I have made allowances for her fancies, including her friendship with you. But enough is enough. You are no longer welcome in this house except at *my* express invitation. You will surely not wish to say anything more in this matter?"

Gilbert bowed his head in silence. Never had he so respected this gaunt, austere old man.

"Very good. We are both gentlemen. And men of the world. The rest, as Hamlet says, if under rather different circumstances, is silence."

He went back to his mother's house, not to reproach her for whatever she might have told his uncle, but to thank her. She brushed this aside.

"I *think*, if you call Olive, she just *might* agree to have dinner with you. Though one can never be sure with a girl of her quality and high standards. But if she does agree, I advise you to waste no time in proposing. And if she will have you, and if you'll take my advice, you'll offer to build her a *modern* house."

3

A little more than a year after the weekend in Tuxedo Park, when Gilbert had taken the resolution to return to his old muse, he was walking around the still-unfinished structure of the Palladian villa on Round Hill Road in Greenwich which he had hoped would be his masterpiece. He had picked a cold Sunday morning in early spring, when neither owners nor builders would be present, to drive out from the city for a solitary inspection and assessment of his work. Yet he had invited someone to join him later that morning. He was hoping that his mother, who was weekending in the neighborhood, would dispel, after one dazzled glance, the murky doubts that had been gathering in a mind depressed since his recent sixtieth birthday.

A black limousine turned off the road and moved slowly, even a bit distrustfully, up the bumpy dirt drive and paused doubtfully before the house. When the chauffeur, evidently not sure that his elderly passenger wished to emerge, did not get out, Gilbert sprang to open the door and lend a hand to his mother. Mrs. Kane, even larger and more splendid in her mid-eighties, grabbed his arm firmly and descended slowly from the car.

"I shan't be long, Fred," she said to her weekend hostess's man. "Just time for a look around." She turned now to face her son's work, straightening herself up for a good look.

The façade seemed to be aware it was under inspection. Gilbert fancied that it, too, was pulling itself to attention. The portico over the front door, supported by two Doric central columns and a pilaster on each end, was the only decoration in the simple red brick front with four green-shuttered windows, two squares on the second story and two oblongs below.

"The Villa Emo," she said at last. "Well, you picked one of my favorites."

"Would you like to go in?"

"I think I'd rather not clamber around, if you don't mind. Let me just sit here and take it in." She settled herself on one of the two marble benches that were waiting to be placed in the garden. "It does rather miss the great plains of northern Italy. But I suppose you must make do with what you have."

Gilbert was faintly irritated. "I thought I'd compensated for that by eliminating the wings. Emo spreads them like a bird, as if to cover the countryside. Instead, I put up the separate guest pavilion over there." He nodded toward the oblong one-story bungalow nearer the road. "I thought the main house by itself would go better with the more consolidated estate planning of Greenwich."

"Well, it looks very well," she conceded. "Any part of Emo, I suppose, would look that."

"It isn't Emo," he retorted, frankly testy now. "Emo just gave me my starting point. You might say it's a dialogue with Emo. A dialogue between my humble self and the great Palladio."

"That's just an architect's fancy talk, my dear. It's Emo to the life."

"You mean it's a copy!"

"Well, let's call it a very fine copy."

"Oh, Mother, that's a terrible thing to say!" His heart seemed suddenly to be burning up inside, a quick spurting flame, as if from paper. In another minute it would be only ashes in a black grate. "And you always used to say that my greatest gift was knowing how to make an original statement out of an old idea!"

"I did. And it was. But that's still just Emo. Why go on about it? I'm sure your client is delighted."

"He is. But I'm not. If this house isn't what I thought it was, after all the labor of the last year, it means I've lost my touch. Touch, hell! It means I've lost my genius!"

"You use such big words, my dear. Can't you be satisfied with a handsome house and a contented client?"

"Must you damn me with quite such faint praise?"

"Well, did you ask me over to give you my opinion or to echo yours?"

He groaned aloud. Of course he had wanted her to confirm his own, or rather to convince him that his doubts were baseless. "Can't you try to be a little more sympathetic when your only son discovers that he has fatally betrayed his truest inspiration? That he has wasted the best years of his life on what he could do with his left and not his right hand?"

"Those old villas were really everything to you?" she asked. There was at last a flicker of sympathy in her tone. "All the wonderful things you've done since, things that have given comfort and pleasure to thousands of people, they all go for nothing now?"

"No, they count. For something, anyway. But I used to have a theory that the god of art gave to a very few favored souls the chance to do something perfect. And if they were faithful to his trust, absolutely faithful, if they sacrificed everything to it, he would reward them with a special ecstasy, an ecstasy unlike any mere mortal happiness, that made up for any failure in the eyes of the world, any poverty or degradation or loneliness."

"You mean they had to be monks?"

"No, no, they could do anything they liked with their lives, so long as the art always came first. But if they betrayed the trust . . . well, woe to them. And now I want *you* to tell me something, Mother, and I want you, please, to be absolutely truthful with me. Don't you sometimes regret that you didn't go on the stage? No matter how small a career you'd have had? And no matter what it might have cost you in the way of family?"

Mrs. Kane seemed now to enter into his mood. She stared blankly ahead of her, as if she were seeking to recall something. "Do you mean," she asked in a different tone, "that if I could see the young Thésée approaching me across the boards, his mind bent only on putting behind him as fast as possible a vexatious interview with an importunate step-mother, and if I could raise my arm to greet him, to delay him, to make him stay some little while if possible . . . ?"

"Yes, yes!" he exclaimed eagerly. "That's it!"

"And, rising from my seat . . . ?" Here she slowly heaved her large body up and stood majestically straight. Raising her arm toward the door of his house, she intoned, in a voice richer and more musical than he had ever heard from her:

> *On dit qu'un prompt départ vous éloigne de nous,*
> *Seigneur. A vos douleurs je vais joindre mes larmes;*
> *Je vous viens pour un fils expliquer mes alarmes.*
> *Mon fils n'a plus de père, et le jour n'est pas loin*
> *Qui de ma mort encore doit le rendre témoin.*

She stopped, shook her head sadly and sat down.

"Yes," she admitted ruefully. "It would have been worth anything."

"Then all you've had since hasn't compensated!" he exclaimed, almost in a tone of triumph.

"It's true. It hasn't."

"Which means that even I, your son, haven't made up for it."

"No, dear child, even you haven't."

"Then we're in the same boat."

"Is that a compensation?"

"I don't know why it should be, but I think it might be. We can get together at special times. I'll show you my old drawings of houses, and you will recite *Phèdre.*"

But now she had returned to her old self. She smiled at him as if he were a fanciful child. Then she turned to signal to the chauffeur that she was coming.

"No, dear, we can never do that."

"And just why not?"

"Because it wouldn't be fair to Olive." She took his arm, and he helped her up. "Your job, you must understand, will be to make very sure that she never hears a word about the silly talk we've been having today. Or even has reason to suspect it. Don't you agree that you owe her at least that?"

POLYHYMNIA

Muse of Sacred Song

THE ARCHBISHOP instructed me to write out this apologia or confession, whatever it may turn out to be — perhaps it will simply end as the plain account of my unhappy situation and its origins — and to begin it on the first day of the then approaching new year, so I am dating this page January 1, 1925.

"Your first love, my dear Reggie Turner, as I well recall, was literature. Before you decided to become a priest, you were all for being a writer. Well, maybe that is just the way to work your problem out. First by putting down on paper exactly what it is. Surely you must recognize that a release from your vows is a very serious matter."

"Even if I'm not fit to be a priest?"

"How can we be sure of that? How old are you? Twenty-nine? Thirty? You have years to reflect, to repent, even to reform. Whatever may be needed."

I stared gloomily at the window behind his desk through which, even closed, we could hear the rumble of Madison

Avenue, almost on our level. The Archbishop's bland round face, surmounting his round tight little body in immaculate black, was, as always, uncannily redeemed from the flesh and the world with which it seemed so linked by the spiritual quality of the small tan eyes he kept steadily fixed on his interlocutor and the set half-smile that mightn't have been a smile at all. I reflected with mortification that he was giving a lot of important time to a most unimportant person.

"If Mrs. Douglas had her way, I'd be burned at the stake in Times Square!"

"That comment is out of order, my son."

His tone was soft, but entirely authoritative. His round little hands were folded on a spotless blotter. Even the crude portraits of his predecessors, stout, smug, irretrievably Celtic, could not derogate from the dignity that emanated from his presence. But *what* have I just written about those wretched portraits? Will I have to show it to him? Yes, of course, I'll have to show it to him. Perhaps that is why I wrote it. How full of hate I am! How could anyone wish me to go on being a priest?

"You are too kind, sir. I have presumed on your patience."

"Your case is a special one, my dear boy. You were not reared to be one of us. You had to break through walls to gain the church. These things must be taken into account. And we must consider, too, how all of this may affect your dear mother. She has always been deeply sympathetic to your vocation. Go in peace, my son. Go in peace and write your piece. You see I can never resist a bad pun. God bless you, my boy!"

Archbishop Walsh's speaking of my mother was characteristic of the whole world in which I grew up. Everyone was always speaking of Mother. Alice and I seemed to exist only as her children, and we were presumably expected to rejoice in the label. If we didn't, it must have been due to our perversity.

Mother, to my childish eyes, was the mistress of a Moorish castle in the middle of a desert of limitless sand. Within, one reclined on silk cushions on divans, breathing in the perfumed air, listening to the lute and waited on by devoted slaves. I might have been something of an anomaly there, being neither a woman nor a eunuch, but Mother cuddled me to her side, fingering my blond curls abstractedly as she issued instructions to menials in her cool clear tone. If I shrank at the idea of ever having to go outside, she would simply laugh her high laugh and exclaim that only a fool would exchange our existence for one of lizards and scorpions.

The fantasy shows how competent an artist Mother was in her own peculiar field, for it was she who had painted my vision. She had converted the dark, bleak mansions that Father had inherited on Fifth Avenue and in Newport into shrines of luxury, but instead of barring her gates to the outer world, she had lured in the threatening warriors and emasculated them at the most Lucullan of dinners.

Mother indeed was no lute-loving houri. She was a mine of energy, a triumphant hostess, a handsome Junoesque figure with hair that was always golden and serene pale blue eyes that saw only what they wished to see. Her aura of calm and repose was a mask that covered a frenetic activity. No detail of housekeeping was beneath her. Her butler and footman in setting the vast dining room table had to equalize the distances between the covers with a ruler, and a single withered petal in the glorious floral display evoked a gentle but immediate reproof. Even on family summer picnics the chauffeur would set up a folding table in the wilderness and place on it the wicker baskets crammed with delicious things. Mother seemed to

regard her very guests as part of the décor of her entertain-
ments. I remember her pausing over a list of invitees to a
garden party and exclaiming with genuine regret: "But I can't
ask Margaret Lee! She might wear that huge ghastly blue hat
she's so stuck on!"

Her guests, however, once qualified, had nothing to com-
plain of, and the society columns lauded her above other hostesses. But on non-party days the big gaudy chambers of our
homes in winter and summer had some of the mournful loneliness of empty theatres, and Alice and I, though usually meek
and accepting, could not but feel ourselves relegated to the
fringes of Mother's busy existence.

It was not that she was ever unkind or even unloving. Quite
the contrary. She was inclined to be demonstratively affectionate and was always insisting that the closeness of our family
ties was a model to all. In the portraits she commissioned of
Alice and me, we were shown with arms intertwined, in laces
and frills, or hugging Mother dramatically on a sofa (this last
by Boldini), as if to proclaim our solidarity and refute the
horrid little facts that crept stubbornly in at the corners of our
lives: Alice's depressions and my own occasional hysterics.

Where was Father in all this? Usually absent at sea on the
yacht that brought him his only satisfaction, where he could
invite a few old cronies to cruise and drink with him. Father
had worked until early middle age in the New York office of
his father's Pittsburgh coke business, and when the latter had
made them both rich by selling the works to Andrew Carnegie, he had found himself with nothing to do, too old to take
up a profession. A moody, brilliant man who had been cap-
tured by my mother's youthful beauty, and bitterly disillusioned by what he deemed her trivial obsession with society,
he had early in our lives absented himself from the family

hearth to find solace in the bottle and on the briny deep. On his rare appearances he was gruff and formal with his children; as a parent he was almost a cipher.

Mother could never understand him. Why could he not be as happy as she in their lovely life with all their lovely friends and the many lovely occasions of entertaining them? What was so wonderful about knocking about on the ocean? She could be almost touching in her pathetic efforts to interest him in her new ideas for parties: musicals, private theatricals, charades, fancy dress. Even when he was abrupt to the point of downright rudeness, she would excuse him to us on the ground that he was tired, or worried about the "market," or simply being as unreasonable "as men will be." She never for a moment faced the fact that love had disappeared from *both* their hearts. Love was good taste, wasn't it?

Mother, as I grew older, didn't shut out the world for me; she lived too much in it. What she did was somehow to establish herself in my mind as a counterbalancing force to the world; there was it and there was Mother; the cosmos was a duality. The two elements were not necessarily antagonistic; they could live together in a kind of harmony with a little good will. Mother's attitude to her co-equal was one of gentle irony, of occasional impatience. When she came up to see me in the large dark Gothic boarding school in New Hampshire to which my father, in a rare exhibition of will, had insisted on sending me, her presence jolted even that fixed routine, from the moment when her huge red-uniformed chauffeur parked her equally fiery Rolls-Royce town car in the headmaster's reserved space by the chapel and she descended, all smiles, to ask that indignant pedagogue whether she could take my dormitory on a picnic. I would suffer agonies of embarrassment at her flouting of all rules governing visiting parents: the beautiful silk tie she brought for my dormitory master, the golden-wrapped chocolates she distributed to the boys, the high voice with which she warbled out of tune the hymns in chapel and the equally high cries with which she cheered the wrong side at the Saturday afternoon football game. Yet even I could see that her intrusions into the set schedules were welcome to the boys and younger masters and that my meagre stock of popularity gained a few points, very temporarily, by the possession of a parent so colorful and bizarre. But convention always won out in the not very long run at Saint Matthew's; Mother once gone, her silliness and not her originality remained to brand me.

I suppose, by the new Freudian rules, I should have turned out a homosexual. Was that not the common fate of the coddled darlings of dominating mothers and abdicating fathers? But such was not to be my fate. The lust that I felt for girls in my late school and Harvard days was one of the elements that propelled me into the arms of the church. For I never developed a reasonable or even a friendly attraction to my contemporaries of the opposite sex. The act of love always appeared to me as a beastly copulation. I have my own amateur theory of what may have gone wrong. It is a truism that boys find it difficult to conceive of their mothers making love, and in my case this could have been even stronger, as Mother, like many society hostesses of her day, may have been what is now called "frigid." Could I not as a child have imagined my own generation by a dark, remote and severe father as a kind of rape? And, in a way, might it not have been? Could this not explain why I tended mentally to brand women who actually *liked* that kind of thing as tramps? And to condemn the solitary and shameful acts with which I relieved my libido as crimes against the maternal half of creation, against Mother herself?

Reserved, timid, of little athletic ability and small appetite for learning, other than what was contained in romantic literature, I was an unprepossessing but largely unnoticed student at Saint Matthew's. For I had taken refuge in a kind of protective coloration to blend into the grey background of that solemn institution. I came almost to enjoy my anonymity and wondered whether I was not beginning to understand why Father spent so much of his life at sea, gazing at the horizon as he stood silently on the bridge, waiting patiently for his ultimate inclusion in the greater and final silence.

In my last year at school, however, I made a friend who changed my life. Or rather whose religion changed my life. I had had a few other friends, boys like myself who tended to be moody and lustreless (Mother said of one of them, after failing to get three words out of him at lunch, that he wouldn't be asked to dinner even to avoid a table of thirteen), but they had had no effect on me. Frank Chappell was a big boy, handsome in a blocky manner, but he was so dull that even his prowess as a football guard hardly made him acceptable to the elite of our class. He didn't, however, bore me at all, probably because it never occurred to me that anyone *could* bore me. He was serious, humorless, thoroughly decent and a Catholic, of a devout New York family.

Saint Matthew's was a strict Episcopal school, but a few Catholic boys were admitted under condition that they attend all chapel services. On Sundays they were allowed to go to early mass in the neighboring village in the bus that took the school maids. Frank's parents knew their son too well to fear the effects on him of any effort to proselytize; the social advantages of the school, to their mind, outweighed its heresy. Nor were they wrong. Frank was resolute in his faith as in everything else. And he never made the least effort to convert me. It was I who came to envy him the consolation of his quiet conviction that his psyche contained a comforting presence evocable at any moment.

The Episcopal Church had never offered me anything like that. Its ceremonies were associated in my mind with the other formal underpinnings of our social life. Mother was a regular churchgoer, and when I watched her kneeling, a bit laboriously, to take communion, greeting her neighbors at the rail with a brief and (for the occasion) democratic nod, glancing up to salute the chalice bearer with the hint of a gracious smile and, after the service, lauding the minister's sermon as he, unctuous with gratification, took her hand in both of his and shook it slowly, it seemed to me another of her parties. There was never the inner certitude, the inner peace and joy that I sensed in Frank. He seemed impregnable, and I came to wonder whether I couldn't be that, too.

The first truly bold act of my life was to ask my dormitory master whether I could go to mass with Frank. He was obviously taken aback; he would have to consult the headmaster. That worldly and formidable old prelate received me in his vast study, hung with photographs of athletic teams, as if I had been guilty of some offense too grave for ordinary discipline, but his tone was uncharacteristically gentle. I must have represented something dangerous, to be caught and stifled as soon as possible. Did he foresee a twentieth-century Oxford Movement sweeping the New England church schools? He would take the matter under advisement; he would write to my parents. Father was fortunately off cruising, and Mother answered with the request that I be sent home to discuss the problem, which was promptly granted.

Mother was not at all hostile to my project; on the contrary it caught her fancy and interest as no other proposition of mine ever had. Until then she had tended to see me, I'm afraid, as a not too individualized offspring through the mists of a warm but not too discriminating maternal affection. She now told me that she had long had a secret hankering for the more splendid rites of the Roman Church, for the soaring choral music, the smell of incense, the intoning priests, the glory of Gothic cathedrals and red-robed cardinals. "They do it so well!" she exclaimed, clasping her hands. She had never dared to "take the leap"; my father and most of her friends were too anti-Catholic, associating the faith with superstitious Irish maidservants and the rough priests who led them by the nose. "But if I had someone to lead the way!" she ended.

Then she really surprised me. "I've arranged for you to talk with Archbishop Walsh."

I shouldn't have been surprised. It was Mother all over, to go straight to the top. The Archbishop of the Roman Catholic diocese of New York was a familiar figure to all. He sat by the mayor at parades; he gave the invocation at political dinners; he was quoted in all the newspapers on the moral aspects of current events and he was as much at home in the grand ballroom of the Waldorf-Astoria as at the altar of Saint Patrick's Cathedral. He was affable, shrewd, worldly wise (would Your Grace object to that?) and universally admired, even by non-Catholics. The social world cultivated him, and Mother placed him on her right at her grandest dinners.

When I called on him in his "palace" behind the cathedral, he was, of course, much too astute to encourage me in anything but the fulfillment of my simple wish.

"Go to mass with your school friend, by all means, my son. And if you find it edifying, as I have no doubt you will, come to mass at the cathedral on your next vacation, and I will give you breakfast afterwards."

I returned to school with the necessary permission and never missed a Sunday mass before my graduation in the spring. And of course I attended services at the cathedral in the Christmas vacation and enjoyed an inspiring breakfast with my new mentor. At school I no longer felt lonely or set apart. However much of an oddball I appeared to my classmates, I was at peace with myself. There may even have been a smugness in my new security, a sense of something like pity for those still benighted. Frank Chappell seemed to find that I was overdoing it; I was encountering for the first but not the last time the irritation that born Catholics feel with zealous converts. I think he was even faintly embarrassed when I announced my intention to be received into the church. Protestants, I fancy he believed, were all very well, but they should stay in their place. He could not have reconciled any such attitude with his faith, but Frank was never one to see that things had to be reconciled. He took the world pretty much as it came.

He went to Yale and I to Harvard, and for the next four years we met only on football weekends or at New York parties. My interests, at any rate, had developed in very different directions from his. I was taking as many courses as I could in English and French literature and trying my hand at pieces for *The Advocate*. There had never been a writer in our family, but I was beginning to wonder whether I shouldn't be the one to break new ground, and I made a special trip to New York to talk with old Mr. William Dean Howells, whom my mother, true to her habit of going straight to the top, had invited to lunch that I might meet him. That dear delightful dean of American letters was enchanting to me. When I told him that I was a fervent convert to the Roman Church, he replied, "Then why not become a fervent Catholic writer?"

This gave me the inspiration that sustained me for the next two years in Cambridge. I was now determined to be a "Catholic novelist," not a novelist who happened to be a member of the faith, but one whose whole work was designed to promote it. I at once proceeded to devote my afternoons to the composition of a story about a reputable banker who finds himself suddenly, even quixotically, involved in a hugely profitable and virtually undiscoverable embezzlement. At the opulent debutante party he is now able to give for his beloved only daughter, he is suddenly seized in the stranglehold of an atrocious depression. He knows at once that he is damned, that he has already, fully alive, descended into hell. In a desperate effort to redeem his soul he seeks to restore the stolen funds to their rightful owners, but each repayment results only in his further enrichment. Nothing will ransom him, it seems, but public confession and exposure, and when he at last resorts to this, he and his family are publicly disgraced and beggared. His ultimate torture was to be his apprehension that it was Satan who had induced him to prefer his own salvation to the welfare of his loved ones, but in the end . . .

Well, I never finished the silly story, so why go on? Reading over my feeble chapters shortly before graduation, I realized what any amateur critic could have told me: that miracles and mystical experiences are interesting only if true, or at least supposed to be true; there is no place for them in fiction. But quite aside from this it was cruelly evident to me that my pages showed no sign of genius, now or yet to come. They were flat and lifeless. I fell into a depression as profound as that of my fictional protagonist. I had to leave college, graduating *in absentia,* and take refuge in the expensive sanatorium to which Mother now sent me, the same that provided her with an occasional retreat when the social whirl proved too hectic.

It was here that Archbishop Walsh took time out from his

busy schedule to visit me. He sat quietly by my bedside, making a few joking remarks about the splendor of my medical establishment. These were followed by a silence that was somehow peaceful rather than constrained. When he next spoke, it was very softly and gravely.

"Your dear mother has told me of your literary aspirations and disappointment. She has even showed me a typescript that her secretary made of your unfinished novel." He raised a hand as I indignantly sat up. "You must forgive her. She meant very well, and I think she did the right thing. Indeed, it may have turned out providentially. It may be that the good Lord has not destined you to be a writer. I cannot tell. I am no literary critic. All I can be sure of is that the young man who wrote those pages wished with all his heart to convey the word of God to his fellow men. Is that not so, my son?"

"I thought it was. But I hadn't the means to do it."

"Perhaps not in fiction. You may have been marked for a higher calling. To convey the word of God more directly. As a priest."

Never shall I forget the immediate, simple conviction that those deliberate words conveyed to me. I could not speak. Then I found that I was trembling all over. My eyes filled with tears. The Archbishop rose and laid a hand on my brow. "It's something to be thought over, my son. Simply thought over for the present. But that is the message I bring you."

Thus it came about that I entered the priesthood. The years at the seminary at Fordham were the happiest and most serene of my life. There was no return of the depression that had vanished with the Archbishop's visit; I had no doubts about my chosen vocation. Indeed, I was so enthusiastic about it that I viewed in the most charitable colors the driest and most boring of my fellow seminarians. Certainly even the best of them, largely of Irish middle- or lower-middle-class background, lacked the easy congeniality of my Harvard classmates, but I disciplined myself to think of the old Reggie Turner as a snotty, spoiled youth whose eyes had been blinded to true merit by the trivial standards of the social world. Indeed, I fell into the error, so common to refugees from Gotham, of attributing nobility of thought to mere simplicity of expression. It is a dangerous error because the inevitable disillusionment is apt to be accompanied by too extreme a reaction.

Mother was delighted by my decision, and I had little doubt that I would now bring her, too, to the faith. Father, on the other hand, was so disagreeable that I felt exempted from the least remorse. He was now a confirmed alcoholic, and his sober times were almost worse than his inebriated ones, for he told me, in a cold, sneering tone: "Your mother wanted to dress you like a girl when you were little, and I prevented her. But now she has you in skirts at last! Maybe it's just as well. At the rate she's going through my money, there'll be barely enough for your sister's dower!"

I had hoped to go abroad, even before we entered the Great War, as a chaplain, with British troops or even French, but the Archbishop had other plans for me.

"You have a persistent romantic streak, my son, that you are not going to find it easy to cope with. The church has no greater concern with war than it does with peace. People are always suffering and dying; that is our business. The exhilaration that you might experience at the front, despite all its horrors, in the vision of courage and endurance would be essentially a romantic one. It is more suited to Reginald Turner, the would-be novelist, than to Father Turner, the priest. Remember that in the trenches Catholics are killing Catholics."

Was it the last remark that evoked my first doubt? Did I

detect a note of Irish hostility to England's war? *Did* I, Your Grace?

"You must learn to temper that exhilaration. You must learn to get on with people even less sophisticated than those whom you encountered at the seminary, uneducated people with vulgar prejudices, people who have never read a book or looked at a work of art and whose sole idea of pleasure is a tavern or a baseball game. I am sending you to Saint Catherine's in Queens. It is a large parish, and you will be one of the vicars."

And for the next three years I labored in a vineyard that was every bit as culturally arid as he had predicted. There were, of course, compensations. I felt on occasion that I had been instrumental in consoling the sick and the dying, and I made some good friends among the older parishioners, particularly the women, in whose simple households I was made welcome. But I never felt I had much success in reaching the young, and my too-intellectual sermons, over which I labored with such excruciating care, were received with the same indifference as the hollow homilies, full of bombast and comminations, of some of my confrères. What troubled me more was the confessional. In the innocence (or inexperience) of my own life, I had had no conception of the rifeness of the vilest sins or of the complacency with which sinners took for granted both the evil in themselves and its facile absolution. It seemed to me that the world was an ocean of malfeasance on whose surface bobbed the few little vessels of the church. What was astonishing was how these small craft were able to give to the sea around them at least a patch of the aspect of a Christian society. It must have been one of God's miracles.

Worst of all, however, in these years was the dulling effect on my spirits of the attitudes of my fellow priests. Few if any of those whom I encountered in my daily work appeared to have much concern with a god of love and mercy. They were dryly dogmatic, wholly absorbed in the outward religious observances of their flock and bristling with hostility to anything that was not Catholic. Indigence and misery in the world around them hardly mattered; so long as heaven was offered to those who observed the rules, was the present condition of things of much importance? Their job was to save as many souls as possible from hell fire, and they accepted with a shrug the conclusion that this goal was not feasible for the greater portion of humanity.

Mother was greatly distressed by my relegation to dreary realms of the city unvisited by herself and was constantly urging me to apply to the Archbishop for a transfer to what she called "civilization." "Don't well-bred persons have souls, too?" she would demand. At last, moved to desperation by my increasing pallor and loss of weight, she offered me the carrot of her own conversion if I would at least tell my troubles to our friend at Saint Patrick's. I could hardly, as a priest, refuse this appeal, and I did as she asked one wintry afternoon in the prelate's reception room, warmed however by the broadness of his smile.

"I shall myself supervise your dear mother's instruction. The angels themselves will sing when Marianne Turner joins the true faith! Oh, of course, I'm aware there are those who think she has lived too much in and for the world, but I believe she has a mission to fulfill, and an important one. And that is where *you* come in, my son. You have labored enough in the desert." His smile now became a beam. "For the time being, that is. None of us can ever be finished with the desert, which is why I wanted you to know the church in *all* its aspects. But now I have a different role for you. Your mother can supply us with a wedge into the stronghold of the heathen. I want a charming and sympathetic Father Turner to be a regular attendant at her dinner parties. You will find that many of the great ladies of the Protestant persuasion are dissatisfied with their humdrum little parsons and are ripe for conversion. It will be your task to offer them a richer, deeper, more consoling faith. But you must do it tactfully and diplomatically. You must never appear the zealous proselytizer. You must manage things so the first step comes from them."

"Not like Saint Paul to the Galatians," I couldn't help muttering.

"What are you saying?"

" 'O foolish Galatians, who hath bewitched you?' "

"But very much like Saint Paul to the Athenians," came my reprimand, now stern. "And it is to people as cultivated as the Athenians that I am sending you. Saint Paul knew there was a time for persuasion and a time for thunder. The work of God must be accomplished with the appropriate tools. The priest in the drawing room and the martyr facing the lions are engaged in the same task."

But I didn't really believe that, and I began even to wonder whether this weighty representative of the church too militant had not suggested to Mother that she offer me her conversion as the price of my going to him. I obeyed, of course. I knew I was in the army. I accepted his offer of an administrative post in the palace with evenings free for the social experiment.

The next two years of my life were dominated by the evening hours. Mother, now a fervent convert, was not only proud but enchanted to have a priestly son as her co-host. My unhappy father had died at last, as was to have been expected, of a liver ailment, and Mother, after a blubbering but perfectly sincere

mourning period of two months (*vide* the queen in *Hamlet*!),
came back, brighter than ever, to resume, however prematurely, her duties as a hostess. No doubt she regarded my new
"mission" as her spiritual exoneration.

Father had been in no condition in his last days to alter, as
he had frequently threatened to do, his will, and Mother found
herself the mistress of the remnants of his fortune. *"Je dépense;
donc je suis,"* she would blithely quote, or misquote, to those
friends who raised their hands at her extravagance. Of course,
I as a cleric had no need of her money, and Alice had married
a wealthy sportsman as lethargic and dull as herself, so I saw
no pressing reason to curb Mother's spending. Obedient to the
Archbishop, I never missed one of her parties, and as she and
I were now asked out as a couple by those who returned her
hospitality, I soon found that I rarely had an evening free.

The Archbishop had predicted that I would be an object
of considerable interest to the ladies of Manhattan society,
regardless of their religious affiliation, and he proved quite
correct. Some of them seemed to be seeking a species of
nondenominational absolution in confiding to a black-robed
dinner partner their peccadilloes. On a second or third encounter these peccadilloes tended to mature into actual sins. Such
revelations were apt to be accompanied by a comment such as:
"I suppose that's a heinous crime in your church, Father,"
uttered sometimes mockingly, sometimes defiantly, always
apprehensively. I would pass it off lightly, but not too lightly.
The door would be left open for further confidences, possibly
even instruction. Other ladies would take pleasure in teasing
or taunting me. "Tell me frankly, Father, are you *always* quite
happy with the church's rule of celibacy?" or "Would you have
to believe the Pope if he pronounced the Earth to be flat?"

I was most at ease at Mother's own parties, for there her

prestige, added to the fact that she, too, was a Catholic, spared me at least the flippancies. And then too, I must confess that the excellence of the maternal arrangements threatened to seduce even my ascetic soul. Mother certainly did her job well. She had "modernized," as she put it, my paternal grandfather's "Egyptian" mansion by stripping its exterior of bas-reliefs of pyramids and sphinxes and its interior of beaded curtains and Turkish corners and substituting, out and in, a kind of French eighteenth-century décor, equally conventional for its time but much less offensive and much more comfortable. The grey panels and green tapestries of the "state" dining room were restful and pleasing to the eye; the cushioned *fauteuils* around the oval table resplendent with pink China Trade porcelains were delightful to sit back in. Father had left a well-stocked cellar, and the four glasses at each cover were constantly refilled with the finest wines, difficult to obtain from bootleggers. It was a double pleasure for those invited to feel that their hostess was as discriminating in the fare she provided as in the selection of her guests.

It was at Mother's that I met Mrs. James Douglas. I knew about her, of course. The Archbishop had briefed me. She was not a subject for my mission, having been converted as a girl in Paris, where she had lived with expatriate parents, and she was known as the leading non-Irish lay Catholic in urban society. But her husband, of rich Pittsburgh origins like my own, had so far declined to come over, although all six of the children were of the true faith and one daughter even a nun.

"Do you suppose she imagines I might succeed where she has failed?" I asked when Mother informed me that Mrs. Douglas had requested to be seated by me at dinner. "But is it likely that I could accomplish what a powerhouse like Mrs. Douglas could not?"

"Perfectly likely. There's nothing a husband resists like a powerhouse. Remaining a heretic is Jamie Douglas's best way of hitting Claire where it hurts."

"And why should he want to do that?"

"I should have thought the confessional, my dear boy, if nothing else, would have taught you that much about marriage."

"I never knew you were such a cynic on the subject!"

"Remember that I was taught by a master."

Claire Douglas, then a woman of sixty, had an air of notable equanimity, unless serenity was the better word. She dressed with the simple neatness and care of one to whom clothes were mere necessaries, incidental to her tall slim figure and the strong features of her long oblong face. It was her eyes that saved her from any imputation of plainness. They were large and calm and opaline; they seemed to encompass you with a patient attention and a mild curiosity, a curiosity, indeed, that might find refuge in dry amusement at your expense. She made me think of a benevolent but slightly detached teacher.

"What is that little pad in the gold clip by your mother's place?" she inquired at the dinner where we met. "She just scribbled something on it. Does she take notes on what her neighbor is telling her? He's an astronomer, isn't he?"

"Oh, yes, he's just discovered something on Mars. Mother always has the latest 'name' on her right. But she's not taking notes on what he's saying. I doubt she's even listening. I know that misty golden expression. Yet the professor is probably perfectly satisfied with it. He will tell his friends tomorrow that Mrs. Turner is much more than a fashionable hostess, that she really cares about the planetary system."

"And she doesn't?"

"Not in the least. That jotted note will be a reminder that

there was too much pepper in the soup or that the Chablis was insufficiently chilled."

Mrs. Douglas nodded in half-amused approval. "So she's always at work. She never rests."

"Some people might think it's taking a party too seriously."

"Well, I'm not one of them. What can your mother do to help matters on Mars? She quite properly sticks to her own trade. Even, which I don't for a minute imply, if she was given only one talent, like the man in the parable, she has not gone and buried it in the earth."

I reflected, with a sudden drop of spirits, that Mrs. Douglas was trying to be nice about a life of which, intellectual as she was reputed to be, she could hardly have a great opinion. And it occurred to me that she might rate a party-going priest with his party-giving parent.

"I sometimes wonder whether I haven't done that with mine. My talent, I mean. Not the coin referred to in the gospel but my aptitude."

"Why, Father Turner, what a thing for a priest to say!"

"I don't mean my talent for the priesthood, if any. I mean as a writer. I tried my hand at a novel once and gave it up as a bad job. Maybe I gave up too soon."

"Why can't you try again? Does your vocation interfere? Cardinal Newman wrote novels."

"But he was a genius. Shouldn't the ordinary man put everything he's got into his chosen profession?"

She responded at once to my earnest glance by adopting a graver tone. "Very possibly. Your calling is not only the highest; it is a most exacting one. When I was a girl I was much taken with the notion of being a concert pianist. And I had a considerable talent, if I say so myself. But marriage came and six children to rear, and that dream departed. However, I have always enjoyed playing when I could."

"Do you ever regret not having done more with your gift?"

"Never. I feel I have done the job I had to do. And the lesser use of my fingers may have quickened my ears. I may have been able to bring to music a more intense appreciation."

"But that's hardly the same as playing to a great audience!"

"Isn't it? Any piece of music requires three persons: a composer, a performer and an audience. Each is indispensable to the art."

"But surely they're not co-equal."

"Why surely? If each is perfect, you have perfection. Perfection must be heaven. Is heaven divisible? I don't think we shall find it so."

"Is God in music and the other arts?"

"Why, of course He is."

"Even if the artist denies Him?"

"God loves beauty. There may even be such a thing as divine greed. He can claim for His own all that's good in a work of art and reject the rest. I hear God in *Parsifal,* even if I lose Him in Wagner."

After dinner, in the library where the gentlemen forgathered for brandy and cigars, I found myself seated by Jamie Douglas. It was not often in the New York society of that day that I enjoyed talking with the husbands of Mother's guests, whose interests were usually confined to business, politics or sport, but Claire's husband seemed quite disposed to discuss any subject I cared to initiate.

His was a strong, fixed presence. His large, bland, expressionless face, which might have been almost handsome with a little light or color, and his large, straight torso seemed to repudiate the triviality of change. Yet for all his stolidity he soon manifested what appeared to be a habit of probing curiosity.

"I knew your father a little," he began. "Our families were

both in coke and bought out by Carnegie. That makes us in America, as the Frogs say, *un peu cousin.* Related by product if not by blood, like the oil and railroad clans. Once or twice removed, perhaps."

"Or even three times in my case. A Roman priest is a long way from the glories of coke."

"As far as all that?" He glanced significantly around the paneled library with its gleaming leatherbound sets.

"Oh, as you see, I visit."

"I couldn't help watching you and my wife talking together at dinner. You seemed so absorbed. May I ask whether you were discussing religion?"

"We were leading up to it, perhaps."

He smiled. "You're putting me off. I know how it is. It's bad form to discuss religion in society. But the subject happens to interest me deeply."

"My dear Mr. Douglas, you can't believe I'm unwilling to discuss religion!"

He took my protest as an invitation. "I envy my wife her faith. My parents were strict Presbyterians. We were Scottish only two generations back. But the black streak in Calvinism always depressed me."

"Surely it has lightened by now."

"Almost too much so. We've gone from faith to good works. From sermons about hell fire to settlement houses. Isn't religion essentially something *within?*"

I wondered whether he had quite escaped that depressing streak from Geneva. If Jamie Douglas had come down from the Highlands of his Scottish forebears to join in the gambols of his fellow men, he may still have left his heart in the rocky Presbyterian crags above.

"One can overdo that, I suppose," I responded. "Like all those early hermits in the Egyptian desert."

"But mightn't they have known joy? I don't know any Presbyterian, or any Protestant for that matter, who feels the *joy* that Claire feels in her religion, the inner peace and serenity. I wonder why I can't have it too."

"Well, of course, you can." But then I remembered the Archbishop's warning about appearing too zealous. Souls, he maintained, had to be *fished* for. "Hell is one of our dogmas, too, you know."

"Yes, but I like what that wise old Parisian, Abbé Mugnier, said: that you don't have to believe anyone's in it."

"Hmm. I wonder. Would God have created something He had no use for? But certainly there's nothing that requires us to believe there are *many* people there. Perhaps only a tiny number."

Mr. Douglas became strangely animated at this. "No, no, that would never do! If there were even one solitary soul languishing there, it would spoil heaven. For how could we go on forever and ever knowing that such suffering existed? You remember that phrase of Shelley's about life staining the white radiance of eternity? Well, that's just what a single damned person would do. No, Father, I doubt I could accept the idea of even an empty hell. For in a time as long as eternity mightn't some poor soul tumble into it?" His earnest expression checked my impulse to smile. Could it possibly be that I didn't *want* this compassionate man to become a Catholic? That I wanted him to remain just as he was? Our old butler came over now to tell me Mother wanted us to join the ladies.

As we rose, Mr. Douglas invited me to a dinner party that he and his wife were giving the following week. He added that he was particularly eager for me to talk to his youngest daughter. I accepted, surprised that the invitation had not come from Mrs. Douglas, who had asked for me as a dinner partner. Had I failed some unexpected test?

2

The Douglases had an old brownstone on a side street, wider than the usual of its kind (five windows in width), probably because Claire, contemptuous of the now-favored derivative Beaux Arts façades, had opted for the peaceful anonymity of the more common urban chocolate. Within, the big rooms harbored a clutter which in the dim light of Manhattan dwellings at first seemed the usual Victorian miscellany but on closer observation revealed itself as an eclectic collection of beautiful things: twisted Renaissance columns, Jacobean portraits of long-legged young nobles, sturdy Majolica platters, black walnut Italian chairs, bronze figures of gods, men and beasts, Della Robbia bas-reliefs, huge old folios spread open on tables and Chinese lacquered cabinets. Claire would sacrifice none of her treasures to the decorator's rule of taste and proportion; she preferred to be able to concentrate on one perfect object at a time to being soothed by even the most harmonious arrangement of the second best.

Mrs. Douglas did not believe in large dinners; she preferred gatherings of eight, where the conversation could be general. But the party to which her husband had invited me was apparently an exception; it was, as their daughter Sandra rather crudely expressed it, the "annual massacre" by which her mother killed off all the people to whom she was socially indebted but whom she did not regard as qualified for her more intimate evenings.

Sandra, by whom I was, as anticipated, seated, was not a pretty young woman. She was short and firmly built and had a set, square-chinned countenance, but there was something appealing, perhaps even sexy, in her intent brown stare and her sharp clear articulation. One felt that she had a fund of passion to offer the right purchaser, if he should ever turn up, which she seemed to doubt.

"I hear you're a great diner-out, Father," was her somewhat aggressive opening. "How can you stand it?"

"You find it so boring?"

"Unutterably so. But perhaps you're looking for converts. Is that it? Are you seeking to stretch that camel's eye for the benighted rich?"

I laughed. "And then steal around behind them to shove them through? I like the idea."

She glanced scornfully around the table. "If heaven is going to be full of the likes of these, it's not for me."

"The state of the soul takes curious shapes, Miss Douglas. But the soul is still there. Surely you believe that?"

"Oh, I suppose I must." She shrugged impatiently. "But I may as well tell you, Father, I found it very hard when my sister Beatrice took the veil. A young healthy woman with a whole rich life before her! I'm afraid I've been in something of a rebel state ever since."

So *that* was what was worrying Mrs. Douglas. "We can't decide for others what will make them happy," I responded in a softer tone. "Your sister may have achieved a peace of mind beyond anything a lay life could have given her. I'm sure your mother sees it in that light."

She pushed her chin forward as she glared at me. "Has Mother ever had a doubt?"

"She is blessed indeed if she hasn't."

"Oh, she always seems to be blessed. Everything goes her way. She's the greatest one for having her cake and eating it. She shudders at the ugliness of Catholic churches here and looks down on Philistine Irish priests, but she can go to Saint

Patrick's, which she condescends to find 'handsome if derivative,' and manages to be confessed by a sophisticated archbishop when she can't find a cardinal. I'm sure it was the beauty and pomp of Catholic churches in France and Italy that converted her."

"But those things can be innocent persuaders. If they help to bring us to the true faith, is that a bad thing? Isn't it better than a fear of damnation?"

"But is it honest, Father?"

"I sometimes think that honesty is the primrose path. I'm sure it is for many Protestants."

"Which is the direction you see me headed, I suppose. No, Father, if I should ever leave the frying pan, it would not be to fall into what makes it fry. What I sometimes think is at least a kind of dishonesty in Mother is the way she cloaks all her pleasures in godliness. When she goes to a concert or picture gallery, or when she's reading poetry or admiring some old temple in Greece, she's never just on an art jag, like anyone else. Oh, no! She's worshipping God."

"And she isn't?"

"Oh, I don't go quite that far." Sandra seemed exasperated that she wasn't making her point. "I guess what I really object to is her impregnability. She does everything she jolly well wants to do. She crams all the beauties of earth in her pocket and looks serenely forward to taking them with her to heaven!"

"But she gave up a career as a concert pianist to rear six children! That hardly smacks of selfishness, if that is what you are attributing to her."

"She was multiplying herself, wasn't she? And we'll never know whether that concert career would have panned out."

"You *are* hard on her. Has her life really been such a bed of roses? She may be properly proud of your sister, but to lose a daughter to so rigorous an order is surely a trial for any mother's heart."

To my shocked surprise Sandra burst out laughing. "That shows you were born a Protestant! No born Catholic priest would admit it was anything but a glory. No Irish one, anyway. And it shows how little you understand Mother. She was enchanted by Beatrice's vocation. What was her loss compared with her child's gain?" She laughed again, this time in a rather nasty tone. "Indeed, one wonders whether there was any real loss at all. If Mother had lived in the seventeenth century, she might have been like that horrible Madame de Sévigné, who conspired with her son-in-law to stuff her poor little granddaughter into a convent to save her dowry for the heir."

"That was a different era."

"How different? Do you know something, Father? I once thought seriously of taking vows myself. Five years ago, when I was eighteen. And do you know what stopped me? I couldn't abide the idea of Mother's pleasure!"

I felt the conversation was getting out of hand. "You have no idea, Miss Douglas, what grief your mother may have suffered under a stoic exterior."

"It's true I don't. But don't think I underestimate her. She may well be one of God's saints. Saints are not overtaxed with human weaknesses, such as family loyalties and ordinary affections. Perhaps that is why they are so often made martyrs."

"Your mother would have been a great one!"

"And how she would have loved it! Can't you see her, clad in white, marching into the arena as the lions roared? Tableau! It would have been the ultimate art. But enough of Mother. There's something I want to ask you. To be perfectly frank, it was why I asked Dad to invite you tonight. Mother, after meeting you, wasn't so sure that you were the right person to

consult. That meant for me you *were*. Well, here goes, before
we have to switch the conversation." She glanced distastefully
towards the stout gentleman on her other side. "It's about a
friend of mine. She wants to marry a divorced man. Is there
any way she can do it with the sanction of the church?"

I was pretty sure now who the "friend" was and why I had
been summoned. Except that my bid had come from her father, whose views on the church were, to say the least, contro-
versial. "Is he a Catholic?"

"They both are. Except she's never been married."

"And was he married in the church?"

"Oh, yes. And to another Catholic."

I shook my head. "I don't see how it can be done, unless he
gets an annulment. Are there grounds?"

"I don't suppose so. There are two children."

"It looks bad."

"But, Father, the happiness of two people depends on it!"

"I didn't make the laws of our church."

We both noticed that her mother was staring down the
table at us. Did she suspect my Protestant antecedents might
weaken my rigor? With a brief nod, she gave us the signal
that the time had come to talk to our other dinner partners.

"I suppose God wants me to yack with the man on my
left," Sandra said sulkily. "Or at least to listen to him, for he
never stops. Anyway, I want to send my friend to talk to you.
Will that be all right?"

I was surprised. "Quite all right, of course. But what is her
name?"

"It isn't she; it's he. Hadn't you guessed that the she was
myself? But you'll know him when you see him. He's an old
friend of yours."

And with this she turned away to leave me to the lady on

my right, who was waiting, I soon discovered, to tell me of another peccadillo.

Early the following morning Mother's old butler knocked on my bedroom door to tell me that a Mr. Chappell was waiting to see me in the library. Frank Chappell! I had seen him off and on in the year that had elapsed since I moved home, but nothing in our renewed relations had led me to suspect his romance with Sandra. I knew, of course, that his marriage to a beautiful debutante, whose selection of him had surprised his friends, had disastrously foundered, and that he had become a disconsolate "extra man" at the larger dinner parties, making up for his taciturnity by his punctuality and availability. But none of this had suggested a great passion.

That day, anyhow, he had the demeanor of a man subject to one. His countenance was wan and grim. "Sandra thought, because of our old friendship, and because it was I who brought you into the church, that you might be persuaded to marry us."

I threw up my hands. "But, Frank, my dear old friend, it's not in my power!"

"You could go to the Archbishop." His tone seemed close to despair. "He could appeal to Rome. To the Pope himself, if necessary. I have plenty of money, now that my father's gone." He paused and then added ominously: "Reggie, you have no conception of what hell my marriage with Annabel has been. If I can't marry Sandra, there's no telling what I may do."

"What do her parents say?"

"Oh, Mrs. Douglas is adamant, as you might imagine. She doesn't even get angry. She simply shakes her head and repeats over and over: 'But, Sandra, darling, you don't seem to under-

stand. He's already married. *Married.* M-A-R-R-I-E-D.' Her old
man is not more help. He seems almost to enjoy the whole
mess. 'To hell with the true and only church,' he tells me the
moment his wife is out of hearing. 'Do what you want. Are
you a man or a mouse?' "

There was a terrible sincerity in Frank's eyes; it put me in
mind of a fire burning in a white enamel stove. His features,
his arms, his body were immobile; everything about him was
the same seemingly lethargic Frank except for that spark in
his pupils.

"Are you thinking of leaving the church? Is Sandra?"

"I believe she might. But do I dare take the responsibility
for her soul? I would for my own. I've already been in hell.
My marriage was that. Oh, Annabel was amiable enough. But
she slept with every man in sight, even the elevator men in
our apartment house. I've heard people say that nymphoma-
niac is a silly term, but how else would you describe Annabel?
She couldn't help herself. She even apologized for it and
begged me to leave her. My faith for a long time was the only
thing that kept me from despair. But when her promiscuity
reached the point where she carelessly left the door open, I had
to divorce her to protect the children. And then Sandra came
into my life, and I began to live again. She not only took care
of me; she looked after my little son and daughter. And now
my church chooses to put a bar between us! Reggie, it doesn't
make sense to me!"

"Nor to me!"

Had *I* said that? My pulse was beating rapidly and my
thoughts seemed to be jumping up and down with my sense
of the passion between him and Sandra. His stolidity, even his
old apathy seemed to have been ignited by her intensity into
a leaping fire. It seared me with a vicarious sexual excitement.

Was it because of my envy, my sick, pulsating, throat-clogging envy, that I had first tried to thrust the cross roughly between them? Was I attracted to Sandra? Or was it even possible that I was attracted to the new Frank? We have now learned from Vienna that anything may exist in the *id*. And worst of all, if the latter supposition were true, might it not have been *that* which led me into the church? We know that God works His will in strange ways, but surely not as strange as that!

He was staring at me. "Did I hear you right?"

"Listen to me, Frank. You say you're willing to take responsibility for your own soul. Very well. You're not consulting *me,* and I'm not advising *you.* But as for Sandra, I believe her marriage in a civil ceremony would be at most a venial sin. It would not be a marriage at all in the eyes of the church, but it would give her complete social respectability. Do I have to say anything more?"

Frank rose and threw his arms around me, hugging me tight. "Not another word, old pal. And you can count on me never to give you away. I'll tell no one but Sandra."

Frank's departure left me in a flurry of agitation. I was glad that I had agreed to accompany Mother on her annual rest cure at Hot Springs. Comfortable in the Mammon of that vast caravanserai while she took her baths, I prayed not for enlightenment but for darkness. But when darkness came at last, it flickered with all the fires of hell.

Frank and Sandra, as I learned after their fatal accident, had decided on a civil ceremony. He had chartered a small plane to fly to Montana, where the ceremony was to be held and where they would afterwards spend their honeymoon on the ranch of a friend. The plane ran off course in a heavy storm and struck the side of a mountain, killing both pilot and passengers.

If the Almighty had used strange methods to get me into the church, was He using even stranger ones to get me out?

Mother really came out of herself for once. Never had she offered me greater sympathy. I was so disturbed that I couldn't even go to the dining room, and she ordered our meals to be served in the sitting room of our suite. She even mixed the cocktails herself, insisting that I needed to be "braced."

"You must try to see this, dear boy, as one of God's mysterious ways of working out His will."

"Very mysterious."

"There are so many things we cannot understand. Why should we expect to understand this?"

"I suppose you think God was saving Frank and Sandra from committing a mortal sin. But what was He saving the pilot from?"

"How do we know? It's like *The Bridge of San Luis Rey.* Maybe it was the right time for all three. Or maybe God was saving someone who was not on that plane at all."

"Who?"

"You, dear child."

I was appalled. I had told Mother, of course, of my conversation with Frank. But could she really believe that God had had *me* in mind?

"Why was I more important to God than Frank and Sandra?"

"Because you're one of His priests. He may have thought it best to save you from the consequences of your advice."

I wondered whether perhaps my greatest mistake had not been in converting Mother. I urged her now to return to her efficacious baths and promised that I would accompany her to the dining room for dinner that night.

When Mother and I returned to New York a week later, I called at the Douglases' and was told that Mrs. Douglas was playing the piano in the drawing room, but that I could go right in.

The piano was at the far end of the room; pausing in the doorway, I could see Claire in profile. It struck me at once that her composure had a marble quality. As she leaned forward to exert greater pressure on the keys for the soaring phrases of the nocturne, she might have been playing in a concert, utterly intent on her rendition, to the exclusion of any awareness of an audience that might or might not be there. I remained rigidly still; there could be no thought of interrupting her. Something in her poise, in the beautiful music she was creating, made me feel that I simply wasn't there, that I had ventured into a space where I didn't exist. It was awesome; I shivered.

When I turned to take my silent leave, I found Jamie in the hall. I had the feeling he had been watching me, but it was always hard to tell much from his motionless face. He followed me to the front door.

"You're not going in?"

"Oh, I couldn't interrupt *that*. Could you?"

He stood very close to me. "You're right. I've never heard her play so well. But then, of course, she's happy."

I stared. "Happy?"

"Her prayers have been answered. Sandra's soul is safe."

I went away without seeing Claire, but I called again very soon and found her at the tea table as witty and delightful as ever. She observed a strict if serene mourning and did not go out, but she was always at home to her friends, and I became a regular visitor. I began to wonder, however, whether it was my oversensitive nature that gave me the faintest impression that her manner with me was less personal than formerly. Now that her daughter's spiritual problem had received its violent solution, could it be that she had no further need of me? Yet there was still her husband to convert. Perhaps she did not deem me the appropriate instrument to bring this about.

She certainly knew I was seeing him. Jamie and I, despite our differences in age, style of living and religion, had developed a curious intimacy since Sandra's death. He had taken a fancy to asking me to lunch with him, once a week, at the Metropolitan Club, where we would sit at his reserved table by a window looking down on General Sherman and his guiding angel and discuss everything from God to crêpe suzettes. He was possessed of an infinite curiosity, sometimes shrewd and probing, sometimes naïve, always accompanied by the same cheerful, mildly defiant boldness, as if it had to be the right of Jamie Douglas, a latter-day doubting Thomas, to ask the universe to explain itself.

As we grew closer, I ventured to ask him to explain *himself*. Why, for example, did a man of such undoubted intelligence not do more in the world than intelligently observe? He didn't in the least resent my inquiry.

"I was in the coke business for a time. I thought it only made sense to keep an eye on my principal source of income. But when I discovered I could hire, for the same salary I was paid, a man of greater economic acumen to keep that same eye on things, I decided to devote myself entirely to pleasure. And don't kid yourself that's an easy task. It can be hard work not to get jaded and fatuous."

"And is viewing the passing world your principal pleasure?"

"What greater?"

"You don't ever feel the need to reproduce what you see? To draw it or write about it? Or at least to comment on it?"

"Oh, but I do. In my own small way. I'll be glad to show you what I've written, if you'd like."

And at our next lunch meeting he brought me two books, both handsomely bound and privately printed. One was a history of the Douglas family, mostly about Jamie's grandfather, the Scottish emigrant, and his rise to riches. It was not much more interesting than other such accounts, but the style was strikingly polished, what is sometimes called Mandarin. The second volume, however, made me really sit up. It was a monograph on El Greco, whose paintings Jamie had studied with a penetrating eye during a recent winter spent in Spain while an astigmatic son was under the treatment of a world-famous Madrid ophthalmologist. It seemed to my dazzled eyes that his descriptions almost rivaled the pictures themselves.

"Where in the world did you ever learn to write like that?" I asked when next we met.

"You really liked it?" His manner was uncharacteristically shy.

"But it's wonderful! The El Greco, I mean. Not that I don't like the other. But the El Greco should be published. It's not right to keep it just for your family and friends."

He hesitated, but when he spoke it was not to comment on my project of publication. "There's something else I'd like you to read, so long as you seem interested. I hadn't meant to show it to anyone, at least until it's finished. But I think I need your opinion. It's a novel. About El Greco."

A perfect copy of Jamie's manuscript (it was like him to have typed it himself) was hand-delivered to me at home that afternoon, and I read it that night. His novella, like the one I am now writing (for more and more, Your Grace, it strikes me so), was cast in the form of a confession, but the confessor, or narrator, was not a humble and erring priest but the great mystical painter, El Greco himself. Jamie had adopted this guise in so masterly a way that before I had finished the first chapter I was nearly prepared to believe that my friend was translating an old manuscript discovered in some rotting chest in a Toledo attic. I knew that his style was polished, but now it had a new life altogether. It sparkled; it crackled; at times it seemed to explode out of the page, so that I almost had to hold it off. I may have been a bit carried away, but I knew, and still know, that I was reading a literary masterpiece.

The narrator of the tale has come to adore his adopted nation. He loves the bare, rolling, yellow-tan countryside and the yellow-brown villages huddled on the hilltops; he revels in the great vistas, the infinite pale blue sky, the Baroque interior of the churches, the bells, the constant toll of bells. But an early brush, however mild, with the Inquisition over his pictorial treatment of the "good" crucified thief — there was a hint of a halo behind his head — has grown with rumination from a small dirty cloud to a darkened firmament. The painter has at first been amused, then intrigued, but later alarmed and at last horrified by the ghoulish machinations of the Holy Office. He becomes a student of their lurid details. He is drawn by a hideous obsession to attend the spectacle of the autos-da-fé, the unwilling witness of tortures which sicken him but that he dares not publicly condemn. His ultimate vision is of a church that has created hell on earth and destroyed the work and word of Christ. This grim message, which can be conveyed only indirectly to eyes capable of piercing the outward signs of his paintings, he secretes in the features and bodies of his subjects and in their agitated backgrounds: in the cold opaque eyes of the Grand Inquisitor, in the flickering stormy sky over a doomed Toledo, in the despairing faces and bare, bony stretched-out arms of the saints, in the fiery greens and scarlets of the annunciations and transfigurations. His agony in the garden becomes the death throe of Rome.

Though it was late when I finished, I telephoned Jamie. He answered immediately, as if he had been waiting by the instrument.

"It's absolutely great!" I gasped. "You must drop everything until you finish it!"

"Are you speaking as a priest?"

"I'm speaking as a reader. Can't a priest love art?"

"Can God be in godlessness?"

"Why not, if He's almighty? Have you shown it to Claire?"

"No, I've been waiting to hear what you would say. I'll show it to her now. Pray for me, Father." He chuckled and hung up.

I was not surprised to receive a telephone call from Claire a few days later. She asked me to come to see her that same afternoon, and when I arrived in the art-filled drawing room, I was again not surprised to find her alone behind the tea tray.

"So you and Jamie have been creating a 'best seller,' " she began in a tone of mild belittlement as she filled my cup. She remembered just how I like it. She remembered everything.

"Jamie has. I don't know why you include me in it."

"Because he was seeking your sanction."

"Surely not as a priest?"

"That's a good question, isn't it?" She looked at me with what I can only describe as a grey gaze.

"I take it you've read the manuscript."

"Oh, yes."

"I suppose you find it heretical."

"I shouldn't dignify it with that term."

"What term would you use?"

"I'd call it a *jeu d'esprit*. A rather petulant one."

I considered this. "I don't know whether it will be a best seller, but it will surely be well reviewed."

"It won't be reviewed at all."

"Why do you say that?"

"Because Jamie has destroyed it."

I jumped up in dismay. My cup smashed to the floor.

"A pity it's the China Trade," she observed dryly. "But let it be. It can be cleaned up later. I'll pour you another cup."

Overcome by her impassiveness, I sat down again. "But that book was a work of art. Was it your idea to destroy it?"

"I certainly suggested it."

"Because you thought it was the work of the devil?"

She shrugged. "Who knows? A great many things can be that. It was certainly full of foolish ideas. But the dangerous thing was the motive behind it. Jamie wanted to hurt me."

I stared. "And why should he have wanted to do that?"

"Because he envies me my faith."

"You convinced him of that?"

"I convinced him that he was wrestling with God!" The serenity of her tone and countenance had now been replaced with something more formidable. "You know the Hopkins poem 'Carrion Comfort'? 'That night, that year of now done darkness I wretch lay wrestling with (my God!) my God.' Well, I hope Jamie's darkness is now done."

"But must a work of art be destroyed for that?"

She glanced with a kind of high triumph about the cluttered room. "Is anything worth an instant's separation from God?"

"I think so. And I shall certainly do everything in my power to persuade Jamie to rewrite his novel!"

Claire became very grave at this. "I doubt he'll even see you now. And I'm very much afraid that you may be under a duty to reconsider your vocation."

3

I sat once again before the Archbishop in his office. My manuscript lay on the blotter of his desk. The plump white hand with the gold ruby ring patted it.

"Well, Mr. Novelist, I've read your tale."

"Why does Your Grace address me so? Do you imply I've made it up?"

"A goodly portion of it, yes. Oh, not the few bare facts, of course. They hardly matter. But the constructions, the interpretations. They are fanciful indeed. I am afraid you are undergoing the crisis of a loss of faith, my son. It is a time of anguish for you. You strike out blindly in self-defense. You don't even spare Mother Church."

"What must I do?"

"Have you prayed? Deeply, deeply prayed? There has to be some answer there."

"I have prayed. And I think I may have made out at least the glimmer of an answer. I need to lose myself in some kind of grinding toil. In some sort of mission to the wilderness. To a savage tribe, the more dangerous, the better. Are there no leper colonies left?"

But he grinned at me. "I could have predicted that. You have a very stubborn streak of the romantic, my son. The devil, we know, is devilishly ingenious. No, I can give you no such easy out. You must humble yourself. I'm sending you back to Queens. To Saint Catherine's. We shall consider our little mission to Protestant Gotham temporarily suspended."

Before I even knew what I was doing I was on my feet. "No!"

His Grace looked down at his fingers. "You forget yourself," he said softly.

"No!"

"Leave me now, my son. Before you are guilty of further insubordination."

"No!"

He hit the little bell on his desk smartly. "Father Turner is going now," he announced quietly to the sister who entered the room.

I went directly home and, slamming my bedroom door, stripped off my cassock and searched the deep closet where I had stored my old suits for what I had once considered my smartest tweed. Putting it hastily on, I defiantly struck a self-consciously debonair pose before the full-length mahogany-framed mirror.

I looked ridiculous.

Hurrying down the corridor, I burst into Mother's dressing room to find her in negligee sitting before her triple mirror while her maid did her perennially golden hair. Taking in my reflection, she said at once:

"Go, Norah, please, and leave me with Mr. Reggie."

That she used the old term by which the household had once addressed me showed she had recognized my change. "What does this mean, Reginald?"

"It means that I've left the church."

"With the Archbishop's sanction?"

"No. With my own."

"But, darling, you can't do that!" Her voice broke into a wail. "Your soul! It's dangerous!"

"Don't believe that nonsense, Mummie. There's nothing they can do to me, even in the next world, if there is one. It certainly won't be theirs."

"Oh, but a renegade priest! It sounds so horrid. Didn't they used to do dreadful things to them? I mean in *this* world."

"Oh, sure, when they had the power. And they'd do it again if they could. Do you remember the nun in *Marmion* who ran off to her lover disguised as his page? They caught her and walled her up for life in stone, feeding her through a niche."

"Oh, Reggie, don't laugh at these things!"

"I'm not." And I wasn't. I was trembling all over. I felt bare, stripped, exposed, inside and out. I was a poor tattered thing. I was a nothing. My only desperate hope was that I was some kind of a *real* nothing. I clenched my teeth to keep them from chattering. I appealed to my Scottish Protestant forebears to keep me from being an ass and a coward to boot. "I'd shout at them the way that renegade nun did: 'Yet fear me from my living tomb, ye vassal slaves of bloody Rome!'"

"Reggie, dear!"

Standing behind her I gripped her shoulders and studied the pale face that stared at mine in the mirror. She had not put on her make-up, and I was appalled at her pallor. I knew she had high blood pressure, but I had not before seen what now struck me as her doom. If I lost Mother, what indeed should I have left?

"Oh, Mum, darling, you and I are going to go right on having the most wonderful time. We'll give the biggest and best parties in town! Let's throw a fancy-dress ball to end all fancy-dress balls to celebrate my freedom!"

"Oh, we couldn't do that."

"Well, we needn't tell people what we're celebrating."

I saw that I had caught her fancy, the only way that was sure. A party. "What kind of fancy dress? Should we give a topic, like a ball at Mary Queen of Scots? Or come as your favorite character in literature? Or anything goes?"

"I think anything goes. I'll be a cardinal!"

"Oh, darling, no!"

"I'm only joking, of course. I'll be the court jester, a fool. And you can be Semiramis."

She frowned. "Dr. Carleton says I shouldn't be up after midnight."

"The ladies, like Cinderella, will be sent home on the stroke of twelve!"

I had a sudden vision of my brother-in-law warning me that, now I was an unemployed layman, it might behoove me to save a remnant of Mother's residue for my future. But wouldn't it be my very redemption to let her blow it all? So that I should have made at least *one* human being happy? And when that was done . . . well, we should see.

CHARITY

Goddess of Our Day

MYRON TOWNSEND believed that his life, or at least the better part of it, had ended on the winter afternoon in 1985 when, in a fit of anger and humiliation, he had flung his resignation from the firm of Townsend, Cox & Collins in the face of the managing partner, Ralph Collins. He had not been obliged to do so. He had survived, technically speaking, what was odiously known in Manhattan legal circles as a "partnership purge." But the price would have been to become a figurehead at a fixed stipend that was slightly less than what the firm paid a first-year law clerk.

Myron, passing through the reception hall on his way home that night and paying what he thought might be his farewell to the three portraits hanging there, wondered grimly whether they did not mark the stages of the decline and fall of the Townsends. His own clear recognition of that seemingly ineluctable process added the final drop to the brew of his bitterness. The large dark canvas that depicted his grandfather Sidney, the firm founder, by Daniel Huntington showed a corpulent gentleman in a Prince Albert with muttonchop whiskers, a man whose god had been created in his own image, one who deemed failure an illness and illness a judgment from on high and who never in a long life had done a stroke of physical exercise. And there was Ezra Townsend, Myron's father, child of the founder's old age, conceived by that fashionable painter John Alexander as the suave adviser to the very rich in the day of the great Theodore, with brooding eyes and a drooping moustache, grey suede gloves held in one hand as if about to take polite leave of a valued but nonetheless tedious client, thin to the point of boniness, elegant, superior, bored. Was he already spending the capital of the family reputation? And answering the courteous but insistent queries of the younger partners with tales of his progenitor's old triumphs at the bar?

And finally there was Myron in a portrait by William Draper, which Myron, *not* the firm, had paid for. Gone now was any suggestion of law or law reports, of elegant oratory in the courtroom or less elegant bargaining in the conference chamber. Myron was seen as tall and finely built with thick, curled, prematurely grey hair at the wheel of his sailing yacht, his handsome profile facing into a marine breeze. And where were the clients? Left at the dock perhaps.

Well, at least there would be no more entries. The worst part of each business day in the last terrible two years had been quitting time. He had come actually to dread the moment when Mrs. Olyphant, his large, bland, elderly, remorselessly smiling secretary, or "executive assistant," as she preferred to style herself, would loom in his doorway, pad in hand, and announce, like a nurse shaking a bottle of despised medicine, "Time for entries, Mr. Townsend!"

When he had started to practice law, it had been the tolerated attitude of both partners and clerks to look down on the allotment of work to hours in the day, to regard the totaling of "chargeable time" as a wart on the fair countenance of a noble profession and to leave the vulgar business of billing to a largely invisible accounting staff supervised by a managing partner whose bizarre enthusiasm for such tedious matters was viewed with outward gratitude and inner contempt. But those were the days when clerks were paid less than stenographers. Now the computer, ruthless seeker-out of escalating overhead, was the powerful searchlight that beamed its deadly ray into every corner of the firm's activities to spy each dusty hour not lubricated with the winking gleam of gain.

"What *did* I do today, Mrs. Olyphant?"

"Well, there was Miss Irwin's codicil."

"Ah, yes, of course. Put in three hours for that."

"I should have thought it was more like one. And you told the dear lady you wouldn't bill her more than a hundred bucks. If you charge her with that much time, you'll have to write most of it off, and accounting will want to know why."

"All right, all right. Put her down for one and charge two to Saint Joseph's Hospital."

"But there's that memo of Mr. Collins's, you know."

"What memo?"

"The one where he said he wanted to review all charitable clients whose hours topped a hundred in any one quarter. We've been putting an awful lot of hours on Saint Joseph's recently."

He knew she meant well. She loved working for a senior partner, and the social reputation of the Townsends appealed to her snobbish if amiable nature. But she knew perfectly how vulnerable he was. More belligerent than he, she believed he should assert his rank and refuse to send in any entries at all, and had so urged him, but so long as he dared not do this, she sought at least to minimize his misrepresentations.

"All right. Put in two hours for Office."

"Under what heading?"

"Just Office General."

She ventured a chuckle. "Isn't there a limit to how much more we can sweep under *that* carpet?"

He laughed in spite of himself. "You mean it's so lumpy now one can hardly walk on it? Very well. Put two hours under the heading of educating associates. I had to explain some things to Nat Danford."

But it was a mistake to have laughed with Mrs. Olyphant. She always took immediate and cheerful advantage of it. "Mr. Collins will be saying that young man should be paying tuition. We've put in more hours for him than a law school semester!"

Her use of "we" showed indeed how much she was on his side, but he suddenly could bear no more. "I'll do them tomorrow," he said testily as he rose.

"But you're behind three days now, sir!"

"Good night, Mrs. Olyphant!"

The end had come with a visit from Ralph Collins, a batch of computer print-outs draped ominously over his arm.

"I've been trying to get hold of you for a week now, Myron. You're a hard man to nail down."

"I've been pretty busy, Ralph."

"Have you now? Well, that's just what I want to talk to you about. A man can be awfully busy without making much money, and if that's the case, perhaps he should change something in his work habits. I've been going over your time sheets and comparing them with the income statements of your department."

Collins, pale, slight and balding, had shining, colorless eyes behind gold-rimmed spectacles. His eyes smiled too much. It was not, Myron surmised, really cruelty; it was hardly even amusement. It was rather the curiosity, quite removed from the irrelevance of either sympathy or dislike, of a scientist performing an interesting experiment. A senior partner who had survived his utility to the firm (if indeed he had ever had any), a representative of Knickerbocker New York, a Wasp, as the current term had it, was being presented with irrefutable evidence that the partnership bearing the name of his father and grandfather was losing more money than could be justified in maintaining his shrunken practice of trusts and estates. What would he say? How would he take it?

"I don't need to see the figures, Ralph," Myron snapped. "I assume they're quite dreadful. I shan't question them. I'll try to run a tighter ship. Next quarter should be better. The Sanford trust accounting should be ready for billing."

"The Sanford trust *has* been billed, Myron. It was billed last year, and the bank has questioned it. I am told we'll be lucky if we get paid half of it, and that will show the matter as a loss. But never mind the individual bills. The fact is, your department has been running in the red for three years now. Ever since the Bradley estate was closed. Do you see any more big estates like that coming in?"

"Well, I suppose there's always my wife's to look forward to," Myron observed, with heavy irony.

"Bella, I'm sure, will bury us all, and let us hope she does! But actually, Myron, didn't you once tell me that the bulk of her money is in trust? And that Milbank Tweed is counsel there?"

"It's true." Myron shrugged, ready now to give up the futile argument. "There'd be only peanuts for us to handle. What do you want, Ralph? To shut down the department? Isn't it an asset to a corporate law firm to have a general practice? How can we call ourselves lawyers if we can't even draw a will?"

"My dear Myron, we can always hire someone to do that. And, anyway, we live in an era of referrals. More and more firms are specializing. What I am finding it very difficult to justify to the younger partners at our weekly lunches (which, incidentally, you have been noticeably avoiding of late) is why you need two associates, two secretaries and an accountant to run a department that appears to be consistently losing money."

"Are there no such things as intangible values?"

"I note they tend to be cited by those who fail to produce tangible ones."

"And the fact that there's been a Townsend in the firm since 1875 — that goes for nothing? How do you know, when a client walks past that door bearing my family's name to consult you about one of his mergers, that he isn't relying, at least in part, on the respectability that my father and grandfather gave the firm?"

"I don't *know*. But I do know that we live in a world that seems to care very little about the past. Everything is now, now, now. Take our balance sheets. The time was when we had to check them only at the end of the year. Then it was quarterly, then monthly, then weekly. And now I find myself asking our controller: Have we had a good *day?*"

"Isn't it all rather hysterical?"

"It is. But it's life. Even the biggest firms live so close to the line these days that with a couple of bad months they have to start thinking of laying people off."

"Well, certainly in estates we've already been cut to the bone. I couldn't run things with one less hand."

"I'm afraid you'll have to, Myron. We're eliminating a clerk, a secretary and the accountant."

"Good God!" Myron jumped to his feet. "You leave me with one lawyer and one girl! Who is going to do the work, I'd like to know?"

"I guess you are, Myron. And I'm afraid that's not all. We're cutting your percentage by a full half."

Myron gaped. "A third-year clerk will be making more than I will!"

"And bringing in more business, too, I'm afraid."

"Very well, Collins. I resign. As of today. And you can take my name off the letterhead. I don't care to have it associated with such a bunch of cheapskates."

Collins's smile was usually a fixed one, not really a smile at all, but now it broadened into a beam. "As to resigning, you must do as you see best. My terms stand if you change your mind. But we're not going to alter the firm name. That Townsend is not you, nor even perhaps your father. It's your grandfather. And I have little doubt that if he were here today, he'd be telling you what I've just told you."

That evening, over a cocktail, in their beautiful long white living room looking down on the East River, he told Arabella of his decision. She listened with her usual air of tranquillity, occasionally turning the thin gold bracelet on her left wrist. She rarely seemed surprised at anything he had to tell her; her small, neat, trim motionless figure, her smooth grey hair and the blue gaze of her calmly appraising eyes seemed ready for any contingency, at least that he might offer. She didn't look her sixty years because she didn't look any age. She was not so much pretty as perfect; her appearance suggested her philosophy of doing the best one could, the very best, with whatever material one had been given.

"Well, of course I think it's wonderful news. I've wanted you to retire for two years now."

"Two years? Why two?"

"Because you haven't had any pleasure in your work for the past two years. Perhaps even more, but I've noticed it only in that time."

Really, she was marvellous! When she seemed least to note she was most noting. In the five years of their marriage she has learned everything there was to know about him, and what had he learned about her that he hadn't already known?

"And what do we do now? Go round and round the world? On your money?"

"On *our* money, silly. But of course we won't do anything so ridiculous. What did Emerson say of travel? That it was taking ruins to ruins? I have a very different plan. One that I've had two years to think about."

Bella's fortune came from her mother, who had got it from hers. You had to go back to her great-grandfather to find the first earning male. This unusual situation, Myron had observed with a wry amusement, had created a curious attitude on her part about money. It was something that only women, trained women, really knew how to handle and spend. Men were apt to hoard it or blow it or dissipate it on things that didn't essentially make them happier.

He and she had lost their first mates to cancer; both had deemed themselves inconsolable. Friends had conspired to bring them together; the compatibility of similar tastes and difficult children (he had a radical daughter, she an alcoholic son) had tightened the initial bond of loneliness, and in their union they had found a life of peacefulness and early hours.

"I've been thinking of the plea you got to head up the fund drive for the Staten Island Zoo," she told him. "Why not take that on? You love that zoo, and now you're going to have the time to do it. I have an idea that you might make a great fund raiser. You've always worried about your ability to make money for yourself. Why not show people that you can make it for others?"

"Bella!" he exclaimed in astonishment. "What an interesting idea! Have you been nursing it for long?"

"I've been waiting till you were ready. And now let's get on with it. I think you're going to need your old office. I'll rent it from Ralph Collins. Don't worry. I'll know how to handle him. And Mrs. Olyphant. She'll be a great hand at this game."

Myron began to feel that a whole wonderful new life was being placed squarely, perhaps even a bit heavily, in his taken-for-granted lap. But mightn't this be what happiness was?

"Bella," he asked in sudden suspicion, "have you been discussing this project with Mrs. Olyphant?"

She simply smiled and suggested that they celebrate the occasion with a rare second cocktail.

2

And so his new life started.

The beginning was simple enough. His offer to take the chairmanship of the major fund drive about to be launched by the Staten Island Zoological Gardens, of whose board he had long been a devoted member, was, needless to say, gratefully accepted, and Ralph Collins, deftly handled by the tactful Bella, was found agreeable to the idea of having a Townsend back in his office at no cost to the firm, indeed, actually paying rent. If Collins was still not wholly convinced of the "intangible values" of an old name, he was perfectly willing to pick up any such values that came free. Mrs. Olyphant, moreover, proved superb and efficient in her new role. Free of the nagging interference of an office manager, she roundly snubbed the secretaries of the younger partners, who had once tossed in her face that their bosses paid for hers. And at the zoo offices, to which she repaired on alternate afternoons, she trained the girls in public relations in how to address rich potential donors — and in how to pronounce their names. Her years of reading the social columns in magazines and evening journals became a distinct asset to the drive.

Myron found that he loved the work. His rich friends and relatives, who had regarded him, a bit ruefully, as too much the easygoing club gentleman to be entrusted with the thorny tax planning of their estates, were delighted to find that they could oblige him by contributing to an institution in which many of them were anyway interested. And Myron did much more than just solicit them. He would take them, one by one, to an excellent lunch in a private dining room in the zoo's administration building, followed by a visit "behind the scenes" to see a baby elephant born or the big cats hosed or a polar bear operated on or whatever the particular event of the day happened to be.

In time he learned to match the exhibition to the particular taste of the visitor. The ladies liked the little furry animals, the more brightly colored birds and the young of almost any species. The men preferred the large dangerous predators. Sometimes Myron, suspecting a sadistic streak, would take a corporation president to see mice eaten by snakes, and for the lewdly inclined the monkeys could always be counted on to copulate. The keepers had been told to produce, if feasible, what Myron asked for, and the only time he had a serious row with the director was when a proposed "spat" between two leopards had got out of control and resulted in the serious mauling of one of the beasts.

The money poured in. Myron was quick to pick up the tricks of his new trade: to get the poorer trustees to pledge more than they could pay (with private assurance they would not be dunned) so that the richer ones would not feel they were being stuck with the whole load; to name the first baby of any species to be born in captivity after a generous lady (with much publicity); to whisper in the ear of one tycoon that another, his particular rival, was pledging twice his sum; to abrogate the names of buildings and wings as soon as the donor's family had become extinct or obscure, so as to have more tags available for new givers; to sell positions on the organizing committees of benefit parties to social climbers and even a seat at Amy Bledsoe's table for twenty-five *g*'s.

Bella herself now took on the job of chairman of a big drive for the Manhattan Gallery of Art, of which she had long been a trustee, and centered her activities in Townsend, Cox & Collins, where she rented an office next to her husband's. "We'll be known as Mr. and Mrs. New York," she said with mock smugness. Ralph Collins's tongue seemed to drip as he noted the passage through the reception hall of some of the biggest names in town. Surely some of these might stick! Myron found himself now invited to the firm lunches he had not dared to attend when he was a nonproducing partner.

It was intoxicating. He had always been deeply mortified by his inability to make big money in a money society, and even when he had, on rare occasions, got his hands on a large fee, he had been haunted by the sense that he had not really earned it, that it had been simply based on a percentage of an estate that had come to the firm through an earlier Townsend.

But now he discovered — or Bella discovered for him (he was happy to give her full credit) — an ability in himself, which nobody could challenge, of raising sums far larger than any partner of his old firm could have dreamed of charging as a fee. He was their equal at last, and it wasn't just because he was Sidney Townsend's grandson, either. Staring boldly at the latter's portrait as he strode through the reception hall, he asked himself with a complaisant sneer who in the world would have given so mean-looking an old codger a blasted nickel no matter what worthy cause he was touting!

Myron and Bella carried their work into the evening hours. She had always been less critical than he of dull parties so long as they were, as she put it, "well done." Ever a keen observer of food, wine, service and décor, the latter including the gowns of her hostess and the lady guests, she was inclined to forgive bad talk for good appearance. And of course, as a museum trustee, she could put up with the fiercest bore if his walls were hung with masterpieces and his table covered with fine porcelain. But now she shared with Myron a single criterion: their hosts had to be wealthy or have wealthy guests. Dinner parties were no longer dull play; they had become stimulating work. Even if they took up every evening in the week, they never palled.

The only difficulty was in not appearing too available to the socially ambitious and thus watering their stock-in-trade.

"I heard you telling Silas Hofritz that we'd be glad to come to his seventieth birthday party," Bella noted in the car as they were returning from a dinner where they had met that particularly odoriferous developer. "When the invitation comes in, I suggest you tell Mrs. Olyphant to call his secretary and say you'd forgotten we were going to the country that day. That will show him we prefer a simple rural excursion to his great gala."

Myron meekly accepted the reproach. "I thought as soon as I'd said it that I might have been going too far."

"A man like that would at once assume that we weren't the real Townsends. That we'd probably changed our name. He thinks his money can buy him anything, and it can, in time, but he's got to put it up first, and plenty of it. That's our job."

"I'll be more careful in future. What is lowlier than an unpaid prostitute?"

Bella ignored his question. She didn't like him to be *quite* so cynical. "We may go to Mr. Hofritz's *next* birthday. Or drop in for a drink and not stay for dinner. In the meanwhile why don't you take him to a zoo lunch? Do the crocodiles ever eat each other? That might be his affair."

"Yet he goes to Amy's."

"That's different. Amy's like royalty. She can afford to have *anybody*."

Amy Bledsoe, who had become an intimate friend of the Townsends, occupied a unique position in Gotham. She had no claim to it in looks or birth. She was an elderly stout woman of middle-class Irish origin who dyed her abundant billowing hair a flaming red and wore large jewels that went oddly with her plain sensible countenance. She had been first the trained nurse, then the housekeeper and at last the wife and widow of Horace Bledsoe, the investment banker, who had left her the "big" half of his estate in a marital deduction trust, the balance going to his son and daughter by an earlier marriage. It was the opinion of those who knew her best that Amy had never been the old man's mistress. She was shrewd, well read, big-hearted and full of sound common sense, and she gave widely and intelligently from her large income. But the peculiar veneration with which she was regarded by the New York social world sprang less from her generosity, which, after all, could easily be topped by multimillionaire friends who could give from principal as well as income, as from her robust character, from her virtuousness (to use a word they never would), from something anyway that made her a kind of saint in a desert that might have been tired of too many lizards and scorpions.

Amy gave generously to both Myron's zoo and Bella's gallery, but when she complained one evening, when he was seated on her right at one of her dinner parties, that her ability to support charities would cease with her death, an idea struck him, and he became for a moment quite tense with concentration.

"You mean because what you have is in trust?"

"Yes. It's what they call a marital deduction trust. It all has to go to Horace's children when I die."

"Who already have millions."

"And who are not renowned, I fear, for their philanthropy."

"But don't you have the power to appoint the trust principal?"

"But that's just a technicality. The law made Horace give me that if the trust was not to be taxed in his estate. I promised him I'd never exercise it, and of course I never will."

"Hmm." Myron's heart was pounding. He even found a moment to reflect that his new idea had made him the superior of his father and grandfather. "Tell me, Amy. Hasn't the principal of your trust gone up in value since Horace's death?"

"Oh, it's more than doubled!"

"Then I suggest that your promise is limited to the date of death value. I can see no reason that you shouldn't feel free to appoint the increase as you see fit. And I'll bet Horace would have agreed."

Amy's mouth fell open as she stared at him. "Why, Myron

Townsend, what a brilliant idea! I see what you mean. It's as if I'd somehow earned that increase. Except of course I didn't. The trustees are two of Horace's most brilliant partners."

"That makes no difference. They were working for you. You can simply add a paragraph to your will that you appoint any percentage of the trust principal that exceeds the value of the trust at your husband's death to . . ."

"The Staten Island Zoological Gardens!" Amy exclaimed, clapping her hands.

Something cautioned him to restrain her. "Or in equal shares to the zoo and Bella's gallery," he added with a laugh, as if to make a jest of it.

"Of course, the children will howl."

"But you won't be there to hear them."

"No, I'll be in the special heaven reserved for the ultra-philanthropic!"

Was she laughing at him? It was hard to tell with Amy. But if she was serious, O gun at sea, O bells that in the steeples be, at first repeat it slow! Myron loved Emily Dickinson. He would raise a hundred million for his and Bella's institutions! He almost regretted now having to divide with Bella. But if Amy were to consult with Bella about the plan, it would be as well to place a carrot under his wife's more scrupulous nose.

And Amy was indeed going to discuss the matter with Bella. That was what she was now telling him, before she had to turn to the man on her left.

"I want you and Bella to stay on for a bit tonight after the others have left."

3

Myron sat after dinner with Bella in an agony of apprehension, the last guest having left, waiting for their hostess, who had briefly excused herself.

"I think I've figured out the greatest common denominator of Amy's group," Bella observed pensively.

"Ambition perhaps? Satisfied ambition?"

"Is ambition ever satisfied? No, I think what makes them different is that they all speak so glowingly of one another."

"Only when they're here, though. The moment they're out of Amy's sight, they tear each other to bits."

"So Amy's is a place of suspended hostilities. That dreadful little new wife of Sam Spatz hadn't the faintest idea who I was tonight, but she bent over backwards to be polite. If you're at Amy's, I guess, you can't be nobody."

"Isn't it possible that they simply want to convince themselves that they really are what they only seem at Amy's? Even the cultural crowd who are on the prowl for grants. Amy cleans them up! For a whole euphoric evening, they can almost forget the wear and tear of acquisition. Going to Amy's for them is like going to church."

"And what is it like for you and Bella?" Amy was standing in the doorway with a scolding smile.

"We don't have to go to church," Myron responded as he rose to greet her. "We're already there. Acolytes at your altar."

She crossed the floor slowly and slumped in the sofa by Bella, contemplating the empty chamber with a sigh of relief. "Thanks for staying on." And she proceeded now to tell the expressionless but attentively listening Bella the details of Myron's proposal.

Bella's face still reflected nothing when Amy finished and sat regarding her inquisitively.

"Will you discuss this with Horace's children?"

"No, because I know what they'd say. They'd say I had no moral right to do it. But I shouldn't care what they thought if I was sure in my own mind that what I was doing was right. What would *you* do, Bella, if you found yourself in my situation?"

"If you put it that way, I have to tell you I wouldn't exercise the power." Bella's tone was light, perhaps a bit self-consciously light. "Not even to deflect a penny from those already overendowed darlings. You're perfectly clear that you wouldn't reduce the principal going to them below its value at Horace's death, aren't you?"

"Oh, of course, that's sacred!"

"And why? Because that was Horace's clearly expressed intent. But didn't he expect that principal to increase in value? Didn't he spend his whole business life making money multiply itself? Didn't he make his smartest partners your trustees? If he had meant you to give any of that anticipated growth to charities, wouldn't he have told you so?"

"Oh, Bella, you're wonderful!" Amy clapped her hands in evident relief. "Of course, you're right as right can be. I have been so worried that maybe it was my *duty* to give some of that money to good causes. My duty to Horace himself! And now of course I see it would be a shocking breach of faith. Oh, my dear, I shall sleep so much better tonight. The whole horrid business has been taken right out of my hands."

Myron was too shocked by the sudden slamming of shutters on so briefly glimpsed a horizon of shimmering beauty to say anything for a minute. He would need time to reflect on the matter. It was better now to make light of it.

"I guess this shows I've spent too much time with my animals. In the jungle one is less burdened with scruples. Everything eats everything!"

"And darling Bella, with her love of beautiful inanimate things, has the more delicate moral sense! Oh, how I see it! But I've kept you poor dears up long enough. You must go home now, and God bless you both!"

Their chauffeur was not separated from them by a glass, so it was natural enough that they should not speak of personal matters, but even so Myron felt sure that Bella was very conscious of the fact that they were not doing so. Even in their apartment they refrained. He simply offered her a cordial good night kiss before retreating to his own room. But then, on an impulse, he turned back.

"Bella. Are you perfectly sure that you gave Amy the right advice tonight?"

Ah, she had been waiting for that! Her eyes were fixed on his. "Perfectly."

"You don't think it's better that all those millions should go to our beloved zoo and gallery than to two arrogant and selfish people, already millionaires several times over?"

"Better? Of course, it would be better. But is that *our* decision? Amy gave her solemn pledge to her husband. I wouldn't urge her to break it to save our institutions from utter ruin!"

"Bella! How can you be that extreme?"

"Because, unlike you, I don't believe that ends, however shining, justify means, however filthy. Because I've seen your eyes grow hard as agates in the last two years. It's my fault, of course. I got you started in this game. But that's just why it's my job to pull you out."

He gazed at her in dismay. "Amy was right. You're as pure as a Ming vase."

"And as hard. Go on. Say it."

"And as hard."

"Perhaps something was left out of my nature. I've always preferred beautiful things to ordinary people. But not, I hope, to beautiful people. And, oh, my dear!" She was actually appealing to him now! "I have thought of you as a beautiful person. I can't bear to have you become an ugly one. Promise me that you won't become an ugly one!"

He stared. "What do you mean?"

"Don't go back to Amy and work on her to change her mind!"

"You think I was planning to?"

"Weren't you?"

The heaviness of his sigh showed that he had given it up. "All right. I won't." He paused. "I'll promise you that I won't. And like Amy I won't break it. Even, as you say, if our institutions should go to hell."

And going now to his room, he decided that he had, after all, married a remarkable woman.

ATHENE

Goddess of the Brave

THE NORTHERN MIGRATION of financial business from the lower end of Manhattan had crowded at lunchtime the restaurants of midtown, and its clubs, once the seats of leisurely, drawn-out meals in quiet, dusky dining halls, were now jammed at noon with hurried, money-discussing eaters. When my law firm moved to Fifth Avenue in 1954 I found myself frequently lunching at the Yale Club and joining in the dark oak bar for a preprandial drink some old classmates whom I had not seen in years. It was on a midwinter noon of the following year that I encountered two of these, Fred Slocum, a psychiatrist, and Andy Ritter, a market analyst, gravely discussing a scandalous story about a third, Alistair Dows, which had just been revealed in a gossip column.

"You read it?" Andy asked gruffly as I joined them.

"My secretary showed it to me just before I left the office. She knows Alistair. We did a will for him."

"Well, you'll probably be probating it soon now. I know I'd blow my brains out if I'd done a thing like that." Andy,

small, sharp and brusque, had always been very much of a no-
nonsense man.

"But would Alistair have the guts to?" Fred Slocum inquired. "Aren't you begging the question?"

That, of course, was the point. The *Amazon,* a cruise ship,
had caught fire in the Caribbean the month before and gone
down with considerable loss of life. Our classmate Alistair
Dows and his wife had escaped in different lifeboats, but
Alistair had saved himself at a heavy price. He was wearing a
woman's fur coat and hat. The story had just been broken by
the writer of "Kiss and Tell" in the *Evening Journal.* It was
such a classic example of cowardice that I could hardly believe
it. It was not like Alistair to be so grotesquely banal. But it
was perfectly true that, with his smallish figure and boyish
face, he could have passed for a woman, and I had already
learned that his wife had moved to her mother's, though for
what reason I had not known.

"I guess I *was* begging the question," Andy replied, with a
shrug. "I always had an idea he was rotten. Rotten to the core,
we now see."

"But, Andy, you can't have known that," I protested.
"None of the rest of us even suspected it. Alistair was the
skipper of an LST in the war. He was in the invasion of
Normandy."

"That's like saying he couldn't be a fag because he's married
and has kids. How do we know what went on on that LST?
Don't forget I've known him longer than you guys. We were
at Saint Ambrose's together."

"And did he show a yellow streak there?"

Ritter wrinkled his nose as if I were being unduly technical.
"He didn't exactly show it, Jonathan, no. His guards were
always up. But I could smell it out, as early as our first year
there. He exuded a faint but unmistakable odor of decadence."

I tried not to look as disgusted as I felt. Andy was like a bloodhound. I could well imagine that he had been one of those ruthless boys dedicated to the mission of uncovering the sore and tender spots of his classmates. I could see him padding back and forth, sniffing the ground with his wide nostrils, and then . . . "You must have a sharp nose. I never smelt a thing."

"Oh, by the time he got to college, he was using a kind of moral deodorant."

Fred, a peacemaker, moved to raise the discussion to a more general plain. "Courage is an odd thing. Is it really courage if there's no fear? The ancients thought so. They believed true valor and fearlessness were the same. *Sans peur et sans reproche.* And they certainly didn't think a pure woman was purer for having to overcome lust. But we still have a touch of the puritan. We feel there should be a struggle. I remember in the war waiting on an airstrip on an atoll with my medical crew for a damaged fighter plane to make a crash landing. The pilot who jumped out of that flaming wreck had a normal pulse! Was he a hero or a psychic curiosity?"

"Do you really suppose Dows had a struggle?" Ritter asked sneeringly. "I'll bet it didn't last more than a couple of seconds."

"Well, whatever he went through, think what he's going through now!" I exclaimed. "Can you imagine a greater hell on earth than having to face the world with *that* on your record? It will dog him to his dying day. His wife seems to have left him. His two daughters will grow up to be ashamed of him. His advertising firm will probably ease him out. What sort of image will he cast for them now?"

"You're breaking my heart," Ritter retorted sourly. "For Pete's sake, the guy deserves anything he gets. He's not only yellow as a banana. He's a murderer, to boot!"

"A murderer?"

"There were women drowned in that wreck, weren't there? And didn't he take a woman's place in the lifeboat?"

"You'd have to show there was a woman on the spot who couldn't squeeze into the boat because he was there."

"There speaks the lawyer! I don't have to show a damn thing. There were female corpses in the water, and he was rowed off dressed as one. That's enough for me."

Our doctor still wished to be objective. "If Alistair were my patient, I'd try to show him there's no such thing as a permanent coward. There's simply a man committing an act of cowardice at a particular time. That might liberate him from the damning label, at least in his own eyes."

At this particular time, anyway, Alistair himself appeared in the doorway. His round pleasant face (we used to call it "cherubic" in college days) was paler than usual, which made his curly red hair seem redder, and his eyes exhibited a mood of sultry defiance. Spotting us, he came straight over and greeted us each by name in a flat tone that had none of his customary buoyancy.

Andy Ritter made no response, but simply picked up his glass and moved away. Fred Slocum responded rather too cheerfully; he gripped Alistair's shoulder and winked at him, then glanced at his watch, announced with an assumed shock of surprise that he had to grab a bite at the buffet before hurrying back to his office, and was off. It was quite possible that in fact he was rushed and simply feared that any inquiry into Alistair's trouble would entail too much time. I picked up my glass.

"If you're not lunching with anyone, how about ordering your drink and taking it to the dining room with me?"

Alistair regarded me quizzically. "Are you being nice or just curious?"

"Both."

"Good. I need to talk to someone."

And indeed he talked right through lunch and afterwards in my office until late in the afternoon. I could justify my loss of working time on the ground that he was a client and that I might well be retained to handle a separation agreement between him and his wife, but my real reason for providing him with a needed ear was neither curiosity nor professional duty, but the simple desire to help in any way I could a friend of whom I had always been particularly fond.

He had never, it was true, seemed equally fond of me. Oh, he had liked me well enough at Yale; he had even implied that he preferred my company to that of the more prominent men on campus whose society he so assiduously cultivated. Why then did he cultivate them? And why did I tolerate a habit so peculiarly unlovable to those it excluded? Because Alistair, however cheerful and outgoing, gave nonetheless the impression of being a sort of indentured servant to an invisible but inexorable taskmaster who was constantly interrupting him in the pursuit of his chosen pleasures to fix his attention on the more serious business of becoming a man of the world, one who would be assisted by the proper friends in taking his rightful place in the financial community, in marrying the right girl and in getting his children into all the right educational establishments and subscription dances.

Well, what was wrong with that? Weren't those the goals of half our Yale classmates? Yes, but Alistair struck me as a charming alien who had flown in from another planet, perhaps as a reluctant spy, or at least observer, and who was being coached by some distant intelligence officer on how to don the garb and adopt the manners of his new companions.

Now, anyway, I learned what that intelligence officer was. For here is the gist of what he told me.

2

If environment were a greater factor than heredity in the form-
ing of our characters, you, Jonathan, would not differ so mark-
edly from your siblings, nor I from mine. But in my case there
may have been a difference between my own early ambiance
and that of my brothers that the "environmentalists" could
pounce on to explain the variation in our personalities. I was
the youngest of four by six years. You know how big and
brawny and tough my brothers were. Of course, it doesn't
show so much now. Time has polished them up, or worn them
down, whichever way you choose to look at it. Anyway,
they're all corporation lawyers. Sorry, Jonathan. No crack intended.

They were away at boarding school in my younger years,
but they were very much present in the long summers at our
lakeside camp in Canada, to which my father came up from
New York on alternate weekends. They spent their days hik-
ing, hunting and fishing, cultivating, even to a silly extent,
the air of the "strong, silent" man, and openly scorning the
distant summer communities of girls, dances, white flannels
and colored blazers. Of course in time I saw them, one by one,
emerge from this state, surreptitiously combing their hair and
donning cleaner pants before borrowing the family launch to
scoot down the lake to some camp where a girl was visiting.
You see, I missed nothing. I had them under constant scru-
tiny.

Father was much like them, a maritime lawyer in town and
an expert, even a rather famous, trout fisherman in the woods,
perfectly content to spend the better part of his vacation days
and nights standing motionless in a stream or sitting alone in
a rowboat. He was a gruff and unceremonious man, utterly

selfish but never unkind. He seemed simply unaware of anything in life but wrecked ships and elusive fish. I am sure he was never unfaithful to Mother, who accepted her minor role in their shared existence with a meekness that probably concealed a nagging resentment.

Ah, poor Mother, you see her at once as the source of all my trouble! And indeed she hugged her youngest to her bosom; there was no holding on to the others once they were of an age to take to the woods. She was thin, pale and apprehensive; her hair was never waved and her simple brown or grey dresses were not only out of fashion — one wondered what fashion they could ever have been in. And yet she enjoyed good health, had plenty of money (even of her own) to spend and had the comforts of a devout faith (her father had been a bishop). Why should she have been afraid of so many things?

She was better in New York. Like many reared in Manhattan, she drew an unreasonable sense of security from the asphalt pavements. But the summers were agony. She hated the great dark forest primeval that surrounded her, infested, as she saw it, with savage and dangerous beasts, the nearest telephone fifty miles away and a doctor's only means of arrival a hydroplane. She would spend the whole day sitting on the porch of her cabin, scarcely pretending to read the book open on her lap, tormented by the vision of accidents that might befall her loved ones in the woods. But needless to say, her husband and three older sons paid not the scantest attention to her pleas that they should not wander too far from the imagined safety of the camp.

So long as I was too young to accompany my brothers on their expeditions, she did not have to fight to keep her "baby" at her side, and I suppose I must have imbibed by a kind of osmosis many of her fears. The two things of which I was most certain by the time I was eight years old were that the world was full of terrifying things and that terror must never be shown. Bees stung; spiders bit (or if not, their horrid crawling on your skin was just as bad); wolves and even raccoons (if rabid) could tear you to pieces; moose might smash your skull with their front hoofs; snapping turtles and who knew what else lurked beneath the deceptively still surface of ponds and lakes. Nor were inanimate things less baneful. Rocks could coalesce into fatal landslides; precipitous mountain slopes could coax you into a fall; and quicksand could swallow you up. Yet from the beginning I had the conviction that these fears were my own personal humiliation and doom. They certainly never visited my father and brothers, and Mother didn't count, being a woman and enviably immune to the jeers and scorn rightly meted out (I always thought it was rightly!) to that unforgivable creature, a coward. I was like a lost soul in a Calvinist world, damned before birth for no fault of my own, but nonetheless contemptible to the suspicious company of the elect.

But there was still a hope. There were early puritans who had clung to the desperate theory that if they could train themselves to *look* elected, they might fool even God into supposing they were. Like one of these, even before my twelfth year I was seeking out those occasions when I might appear brave, or at least normally undaunted, to the male members of my family. I insisted now on accompanying my brothers on their hikes and adventures, tearing myself away, with the brutality of desperation, from my pathetically protesting mother. At first they were reluctant to take me, saying that I would lag behind and be a nuisance, but Father, emerging for once from his personal reveries, told them brusquely that I was to be included, and after much grumbling, but seeing that I really tried to keep up with them, they became good-natured enough.

And I was successful. Or did I have the devil's own luck? When on a camping trip, sitting around the fire at night, I asked what the small illuminated discs in the woods around us were and was told they were wolves, I took for granted that my brothers, as they often did, were trying to frighten me and continued imperturbably to toast marshmallows. Actually they were wolves, whose not uncommon practice it was to wait until the campers retired and then sniff around the extinguished fire for any remnants of food. But I received the approval of my slyly watching companions, though had I known the truth I might have had a convulsion. And another time, when we were climbing a steep hill, the wind carried off the favorite cap of my oldest brother and it landed on a ledge below so narrow that only I was of a size to be able to clamber out to retrieve it. What the others could not see from their distance but was perfectly clear to me when I approached it was that the ledge was actually wide enough to be negotiated without risk. And I was the hero of the hour.

At Saint Ambrose's, the Episcopal Church boarding school near Boston to which all Dowses were sent, I found my formmates, with one exception, even easier to take in than my brothers. I was a good-looking boy, if I say so myself, and I have often been told that I have a pleasant and amicable manner, so making friends was never a problem. But boys can be horribly mean, and they like to test one another, and when I found myself the target of a nasty little clique, and it was obviously necessary for me to challenge one of them to a fistfight in the accepted arena of the schoolhouse cellar, I picked one bigger than myself, but who, after careful observation, I had concluded was a bully and a coward. I had learned by then, you see, that I was not the only member of the unelected. In our combat I rushed at him with desperation and gave him so smart a blow on the nose that he bled alarm-

ingly and quit the struggle. He was known for months thereafter as Attila, who, as no doubt you're aware, died of a nose
bleed. This established my martial respectability, but I was
always very careful to avoid any offense, or even the appearance
of one, that might have led to another encounter.

For I never lost mind of the slender grounds on which my
immunity rested. The school placed great emphasis on man-
liness, not only in sports but in all aspects of life, and it began
to seem to me that even the least eventful career offered so
many tests that I was bound to be found out in the end. Much
was made of the sacrifice of the young graduates who had lost
their lives in the First World War, and on Armistice Day we
turned in chapel to face the great west window dedicated to
their memory and sang heartily the school hymn, to which a
special stanza reciting their heroism had been appended. My
father had served in the trenches, but he had always refused to
discuss his experiences, stating in his usual terse fashion that
there was no need to put in our minds the terrible pictures of
which he wished his own were free. That, of course, made it
worse for me. I had nightmares about those slimy dugouts,
with rats below and death above and the hideous possibility of
becoming a living torso without limbs or being left with a
face that was no face. War would be the ultimate test. There
had been one for Father, and I had little doubt there would be
one for me. How right I was!

I was never tempted to confide my anxieties to a friend. It
never occurred to me that there could be anyone who would
not have deemed them shameful. But there was one boy at
school whom I suspected of suspecting me. It was Andy Ritter, the same who turned away from me at the bar before
lunch. Andy was the predator for whom I was the natural
prey. Like the lion who seems actually angry at the poor zebra

he is mauling, he was always hostile, and my efforts to disarm him, of which I'm ashamed to admit there were several, only made him worse.

"I don't make friends with fairies," he once snarled at me.

Now why did he call me that? I had had no such relations with other boys at school, nor had I even wanted to. I could only assume that Andy was using the term simply in the sense of an effeminate man, and weren't such men notoriously supposed to be cowardly? So Andy *knew*. It justified my gloomy suspicion that I might be able to fool some of the people some of the time, but never "God," whoever or whatever He was, some bearded Jehovah perhaps. For had He not sent a militant angel in the form of Ritter to notify me that my game of *looking* like one of the elect had not taken *Him* in? No, not for an instant.

Andy's attitude, anyway, brings me to the subject of girls, in which I was always very much interested. I admired girls, as did most boys, and I was attracted to them, as were most, but, decidedly unlike the majority of my sex, I also envied them. Girls did not have to be brave. Indeed, the very opposite was true. If they screamed at the sight of a mouse, or recoiled in horror before a garter snake, it was considered actually appealing. I think in some perverted fashion I may have thought that the closer I got to a girl, even to the ultimate closeness, and the more I made her mine, or myself hers, the nearer I came to achieving her blessed immunity.

I tended at holiday dances to cut in on the less attractive girls. It might have been an inner obedience to the saying that only the brave deserve the fair. But I suspect it was more the fact that the males of most species prove their prowess by fighting over females. I remember a diorama at a natural history museum which showed two magnificent bull moose locked in a perhaps fatal combat while the desired cow stood indifferently by, chewing her cud. It was true that the cow was ugly, but male animals are indifferent to age or looks in the weaker sex. Not so man. What the bull seeks is a harem; what the man looks for is beauty. And as I avoided combat, I also avoided its occasions.

Of course, the animals are quite right. Beauty has nothing to do with sexiness in a woman. I met Amanda at a debutante party in the spring vacation of freshman year; we became secretly engaged the next year, and you will recall that we were married immediately after graduation. Amanda was a plain little Jenny Wren, but she was bright and animated, and she became actually pretty with the self-assurance that possession of a steady beau gave her. She had never expected to appeal to a man as attractive as me. Am I sounding vain? But you must admit I was kind of cute back then. You understand that I use the term *cute* to avoid the hubris of claiming I was a man, that is, a warrior. Oh, it's all too clear! But Amanda, God help her, loved me, and I reveled in her love. We were happy, and we might still have been, had we not taken that fatal cruise to celebrate our fifteenth wedding anniversary.

The war came right after the birth of our first daughter. Of course, I had always known it was coming. In the endless discussions with friends of which branch of which service one should apply for, to demonstrate one's proper patriotism or at least to escape the ignominy of the draft, I had considered army or navy intelligence, but had rejected the idea because, I think, I was more afraid of the stigma of noncombat duty than combat itself. Indeed, for the first time I began actually to ponder the possible truth of President Roosevelt's "nothing to fear but fear itself." Was it even conceivable that the war might offer me a deliverance from the apprehensions of a lifetime?

At last I applied for the commission of ensign (deck volunteer general) and became a "ninety-day wonder" after training for that period of time aboard the U.S.S. *Prairie State,* moored in the Hudson on the upper west bank of Manhattan.

And then my fate took a curious turn. Instead of being sent to sea, I was assigned to Vice Admiral Clarke's staff at 90 Church Street, where I found myself a kind of personal secretary to the old man, running errands, writing letters, accompanying him on social occasions and even handling some of the delicate problems of his rather difficult children. It was no fault of mine that he became so dependent on me that he opposed my transfer to more active duty, and Amanda, delighted to have me home, argued strongly that it was a quite sufficient contribution to the war effort to guard from distracting botherations the high officer who was responsible for the safety of our whole eastern sea frontier. But as I had always concentrated on looking the part of a man of courage, it now surely behooved me not to look the part of his opposite, and I suspected that few of my friends appreciated the stranglehold that my chief had on my naval career and deemed me the willing and complaisant captive of his personal needs. And so I found myself in the position of having actually to throw away the shield that a kind fate seemed to be interposing between me and my old nemesis!

The call for more officers on sea duty was now so urgent that Admiral Clarke was obliged to endorse my application for assignment to the amphibious fleet. I had decided that I might do better on a ship such as an LST, where one had only, so to speak, to follow the leader in a line of transports, than on an attacking destroyer, where any moment of panic might paralyze the brain and endanger the vessel. What I had not counted on was the favoritism of my admiral, who followed my career from his desk in Church Street (as a naval officer he could not really resent my desertion) and was instrumental in my being made captain of a landing ship tanks.

Well, it started off well enough. I had nine officers and a hundred men under me, and being reasonable in my expectations of them and polite and friendly in my dealings, I soon found myself popular. We crossed the Atlantic to take part in the invasion of Normandy and had the good luck to unload our troops on one of the less guarded sectors of the beaches. After returning to the Solent three days later and dropping the hook exactly in our assigned position, I wondered whether the murky god of my adolescence had not been appeased at last.

Alas, he was only waiting for a more opportune moment. Some weeks later, ordered to London to take on Canadian troops, we passed at night through the Straits of Dover within range for some hours of the German shore batteries. They opened up on the convoy, and despite the British jamming of their radar, they managed to hit the merchant vessel directly ahead of us.

Now I learned what hell is. My crew, of course, were at their battle stations, and I at mine on the bridge with the officer of the deck, the executive officer, the chief quartermaster and a signalman. The night was black but lit with the flare of gunfire and the blazing wreck of the merchant ship, which we now had to pass and leave astern. I was suddenly absolutely convinced that we were going to be struck. The shell would land directly on the bridge itself. There was no doubt in my mind; it was the simplest and grimmest of facts. I opened my mouth to suggest some kind of evasive maneuver to the exec, whose figure I could just make out in the darkness, but no sound emerged. And then I knew that the horror choking me was simply unbearable. Anything, even death was preferable.

Suddenly I was walking aft. I was leaving the bridge. Leaving my battle station without even transferring the "conn" to the exec! I think I meant to jump off the ship. At least I can recall leaning over the side on the stern, vaguely aware of the staring white faces of the gun crew of the three-inch fifty close beside me, and peering into the hissing foam of our wake. Did I hope to be picked up by a lifeboat of survivors from the wreck astern? Was I deterred by the apprehension of being sucked into our screws and cut to bits? I am not sure.

All I know is that I remained there, a miserable shivering wretch, until the firing ceased and I returned to the bridge. I mumbled something about an attack of the "trots." Nobody said anything.

So there it was. Nemesis. The final blow had fallen at last. Yet in the next days nothing happened. I was treated in the wardroom with the same good manners, and I began to wonder whether it was my imagination that these now veiled an unspoken scorn. I knew that the episode must have been discussed by every man on that vessel. But only in the eyes of the exec, a strange saturnine fellow in whom I fancied I could detect a resemblance to Andy Ritter, did I really believe I could make out a glimmer of contempt, and I suspected him of having felt that for me all along.

At last I realized something about LSTs. The ship's company does not depend on the guts and skill of the commanding officer to anything like the degree it does on vessels of attack. These big naval marine trucks perform their semi-automatic tasks under the orders of a group or flotilla commander, who is apt to be a competent and almost certainly courageous regular navy officer. The skipper of the individual unit is important to his crew largely because of his power to make their lives uncomfortable. If they have the good fortune to have drawn a reasonably easygoing and pleasant captain, how much does it matter if he has a yellow streak? The vessel, anyway, is rarely under direct attack.

So my defection was overlooked if not forgotten. I even dared to draw a breath of something like relief at the idea that the worst was now over. When we returned to the States, after some months of uneventful Channel ferrying, for an overhaul in the Brooklyn Navy Yard, I was generous in granting liberty to the crew and entertained the officers on several occasions at night clubs.

I was still afraid, however, that one of the officers might tell Amanda of the horrid incident. The exec had left us to take command of another LST, and I did not believe that any of the friendly junior officers would do so vile a thing consciously, but we drank a good deal at our parties, and I could not be sure what distorted joke might emerge from the lips of a young and intoxicated ensign. I decided at last it would be safer to give her my own version of what had happened.

She listened closely and without interrupting. She did not seem surprised. But also she did not minimize it.

"It could have been a good deal worse," was her first comment. "If the ship had been hit while you were away from the bridge, I suppose you might have been in some sort of official trouble. Anyhow, you're due now for shore duty. And with any luck the war should be over before you go back to sea."

I did not at all like her implication that the episode was apt to be repeated. "But even if I should go back to sea," I protested, "there's no reason to assume I'd have another attack of nerves. I have a funny gut feeling that this was the kind of thing that always *was* going to happen to me, but now it's happened, it may not come again."

"But why risk it? You're home, my darling, and you're safe, thank God. I'm sure Admiral Clarke will be tickled pink to have you back in your old slot. And he won't let you go again, either. Oh, Ally, don't tempt fate! You've done your bit. Let well enough alone."

But I felt trivialized. There was a distinct discomfort in her minimization of a lifetime's trial. If my ancient inner enemy had been merely something that could be kept at bay by a silly staff job in Church Street, what did the long agony of my resistance amount to?

"I wonder whether I shan't apply for an LST command in the Pacific," I said moodily. "The war there may go on for years."

"You might stop to consider what you owe me and the baby," she said in a sharper tone. But then her expression suddenly changed, and she struck a deeper note. She even stretched out her arms to me. "Oh, my dearest, do you think I don't *know?*"

"Know what?" I did not rush to her arms. Every part of me was throbbing with alarm.

"Know everything, of course. How could I not, loving you as I do? Don't you see, that's got to be the answer? Oh, my poor suffering sweet, if you could only relax and love and let yourself be loved, how easily things would work themselves out! All your bad dreams would fade away, and you and I would be afraid of nothing in the world."

So there it was, Jonathan. A woman's answer to everything. Open the floodgates and let the dammed-up sentiment come thundering out to obliterate all the ugly-bugly things in the big bad universe. And she may have been right, too. That's the sorry part. She may have been offering me my last clear chance. And I, like the ass I was doomed to be, or had doomed myself to be, had to turn away from her appeal. Perhaps I felt that otherwise I should be giving up my soul or my ego or even, silly as it sounds, my manhood. When all she was asking was that I give up the foolish little comedy that I had been making of my life! The absurd little piece that I had been desperately trying to turn into a noble tragedy! But lives that won't bow to a hurricane can bend to a gust of wind. Maybe what I couldn't bear was being called "my poor suffering sweet."

Anyway, I mixed her a cocktail and we changed the subject. That night we made love. The next day brought the news of the bombing of Hiroshima, and we knew that I should not have to go to sea again. I remember my gall in reminding myself, as a way of putting the whole matter behind me, of Gibbon's statement that the courage of a soldier is the cheapest and most common quality of human nature.

3

Alistair and I sat in silence for a minute in my office after he had finished. The room was darkening in the winter twilight. I switched on my desk lamp.

"But you and Amanda had another ten years of happy married life after that, did you not?"

"Oh, yes." He spoke in a tone of faint weariness. "She was never a nag. She didn't return to the subject. As you know, we had another daughter." He smiled wryly. "Born nine months after that discussion. We went on as before. Ours was what you might call a temperate union. Only, of course, because I made it that way. She would have been pleased with something a good deal hotter. But she was always a good sport."

"Until now?"

"Well, who could blame her for leaving me *now?* Hadn't she offered me a way out? Hadn't she given me fair warning?"

He rose and walked to the window. No longer facing him, I was able to be more personal.

"Were there other incidents of your old trouble in the last years?"

"No. It may have been just coincidence. Our life was a very safe one. And my suspicion that I might have finally licked my old demon grew almost to a conviction. We had prospered. The girls were fine girls. We had many friends. The years glided by gracefully enough. And then Amanda and I had to go and sign on for that fateful cruise."

"Did you have any apprehensions before the wreck?"

"I did." He turned back to me, flat of tone and positive again. "We gave a little going-away party in our cabin before the boat sailed. You remember, it was our anniversary, and half a dozen friends had come to see us off. I was feeling nothing but the pleasantness of the occasion when a sudden fit of blind panic struck me. As in the Dover Straits I was absolutely convinced that the ship was doomed to sink. I couldn't even speak. I simply stood there, a glass in my hand, my mouth gaping, until someone asked me whether I was all right. I muttered something about needing a breath of air and went out on deck. Amanda at once followed me. She had been watching me and had divined what was wrong. She told me, very firmly, that we would leave the ship as soon as our guests had gone. But I rejected her proposal. I did so sharply, testily. I insisted that I had simply had a moment of dizziness. There was nothing she could do. An hour later we sailed."

He sat down and we were silent for another minute.

"I'll spare you the horrors of the fire. I told Amanda to go to her lifeboat station and she did. I saw that there wouldn't be enough boats for all. Half couldn't be launched because of the listing. I had made up my mind to jump in the water and was hurrying down the deck when through the open door of an outside cabin I spied a woman's fur coat and hat hanging on a peg. The fit hit me again, and I went black."

He ran both hands through his hair and actually smiled.

"So there we are, Jonathan. There's a kind of peace in having touched bottom. I don't ever have to pretend again. At the cost of everything I valued in life — or should have valued — my family, my job, my friends, my reputation — I have been given back my life itself. And what's more, it's a life so poor and shabby that almost anything I do with it will be an improvement. I'll be alone in the world, but that may be better than to be the way I was."

"You won't be quite alone," I assured him.

"Well, I know I can count on you. And there'll be those who pity me and those who want to show their magnanimity by not dropping me altogether. But I don't think I'm really going to mind being more with myself. So many of my old friends were really friends of the *other* Alistair Dows."

"Perhaps I can tell you something about the new Alistair. I shouldn't be surprised if he turns out to be brave as a lion!"

"What a romantic you are, Jonathan. But the point, don't you see, is that that doesn't matter to me anymore. Whatever I am, I am. And whatever I was, I was. I've been dealt a hand, like everyone else. It happens to be a very bad one. In fact, I don't see any honor cards. But I have to play it out. That's all."

He rose now to take his leave.

"Amanda will come back to you."

"It's not impossible. She may find that she, too, has no face cards. But whichever way she decides, it's all right with me. As I say, I can't go any further down. And I think I can face anything now. Even forgiveness."